Beneath the Surface

Kate Sherwood

Copyright 2019 by Kate Sherwood

Published by Kate Sherwood

Cover Art by LC Chase

Print ISBN #978-1-988752-25-9
ebook ISBN# 978-1-988752-26-6

Second Edition Issued 2019

CHAPTER ONE

THE community hall was packed when Caleb Sinclair edged through the propped-open doorway. It was early spring and the night air was still cool, almost cold, but too little of it was getting inside; the place was stifling. The windows, above eye-level in the high-ceilinged room, hadn't been opened in living memory. Caleb pulled his jacket off and noticed that the buzz of conversation in the room was more subdued than it had been just moments before. Then the volume flared up again, and he winced at the familiar pattern, the surprised quiet followed by the catty gossip.

He turned to his friend Matt, standing hesitantly beside him, and forced a grin onto his face. "At least this time they're staring at you, not me."

But Matt Dean was used to being the town's golden boy, and apparently he wasn't ready to joke about the change in his fortune. "Maybe I should leave," he suggested quietly.

"Why?" Caleb demanded. "It's your town as much as theirs, right?" He waited, then raised an eyebrow, reminding Matt that the choice of words wasn't accidental. When Caleb had come out of the closet, Matt had stood by him without question or hesitation, and had given more pep talks than anyone should ever be asked to. Caleb was more than happy to return the favor of friendship now. "Besides, it's not your fault. It's not even your parents' fault."

"I don't think many of the people here agree with you on

that."

"Bullshit." Caleb looked around the overcrowded room; he didn't think they had a chance of finding seats, but he hoped they could find somewhere to stand, somewhere farther from the exit Matt seemed so eager to use. "The bitchy ones are the loudest, but that doesn't mean they're the biggest group. Besides, nothing's decided yet. That's the whole point of the meeting."

Matt didn't look convinced, but he trailed along as Caleb led the way to the back corner of the room. They edged in next to Mr. Shackleton, who had taught them both geography years ago in high school, and nodded a greeting as a thin, past-middle-age woman made her way onto the low stage at the front of the room. Hazel McAllister, the mayor. She fumbled with the microphone, then cleared her voice and spoke to the quieting crowd.

"Thank you all for coming out tonight. I know you have some concerns, and I have some concerns, as well. But hopefully we can get some information here, and at least have a better idea of what's going on. What's being proposed."

The mayor looked over toward the small group of strangers sitting in the front row. Caleb couldn't see their faces, but their backs were almost uniform—conservative haircuts and white collars just showing above dark business suits. There was one woman with them; her dark hair was coiled into a bun and she was also wearing a sedate jacket, although it was in a rich cream color. Caleb looked around at the rest of the crowd and saw the familiar baseball caps and cowboy hats, the shaggy hair above worn work shirts, and almost smiled. It was pretty damned obvious who the outsiders were. He glanced over toward Matt; he'd had the sense to dress casually, at least. Italian loafers instead of work boots, but that was probably just as well. It had been a long time since Matt had worked on a farm, and everyone in the room knew it. They wouldn't have appreciated it if they'd thought he was wearing a costume.

And how stupid was it that Caleb had to worry about that? That *Matt* had to worry about it? Matt Dean, a local boy who'd left town only long enough to get his medical degree before returning to help address the area's critical doctor shortage.... Matt had to worry about how he was presenting himself to the community. He had to prove himself to the people he'd grown up with.

For the first time, Caleb wondered whether he was doing Matt a favor, standing by him. Was Matt's friendship with the community's only openly gay man just one more way that Matt was defying community values?

Then one of the well-dressed men from the front row stood up and started for the stage. His shoulders were a little distracting: broad, almost rangy, tapering to a slim waist and tight ass. His suit fit so well it must have been custom-made. Or else bought at a store that specialized in dressing superheroes. Clark Kent and this guy would be the store's main clients. And then the man turned around, and Caleb forgot all about the shoulders.

He *was* a superhero. He had to be. Nobody was that good-looking in real life; nobody had a jaw that chiselled, or eyes that blue. Maybe in Hollywood, but not in Rocky Creek, Ontario.

The man's smile wasn't wide, didn't seem overdone, but Caleb felt its warmth like a fire on a cold day. And his voice had just the right tone, deep and strong, as he said, "On behalf of Caplan International, thank you for coming to meet with us. My name is Peter Carr, and I'm really happy to be here in Rocky Creek. It's a beautiful part of the country, and I can absolutely understand why you're all so worried about protecting it. I hope that when we're done here, you'll agree with us that our project is not the threat it has initially appeared to be."

There was a stir in the crowd as people turned to their neighbors to discuss this new wrinkle. More than a few women already looked convinced, and the men seemed a little more favorably disposed as well. Peter Carr didn't just look the right way, he also said the right things.

Caleb was mostly just glad that the crowd's attention was off Matt; the rest of the night would unfold as it would, and Caleb could return to his favorite position: unnoticed on the sideline. With the trouble he was having keeping himself from staring at the beautiful man in front of the room, it was just as well that he wasn't being observed too closely.

Carr waited for the crowd to settle down, then continued. "We've got a lot of experts here to talk to you today, and I think their information is important. I think it's essential that you all understand that we're not just charging into this. We've done our homework, we're being careful, and we know what we're doing. But I think the other important thing about meetings like this is for us to make it clear that we're not faceless monsters attacking you from the city. We're people too. We have families, and places that we love, and we understand your concerns. We do." He seemed so sincere, so kind. His smile was gentle, and he let the audience buzz a little before resuming at just the right time. "So I'm going to turn the stage over to the experts. We've got... well, there's a lot of engineers. Sorry about that." He grinned at the men in the front row as if sharing an old joke. "But there's also an economist, and an ecologist... I'm a lawyer, but I don't really"—another quick grin—"I don't really do *lawyer* stuff, if that makes sense. It's my job to make sure we're not breaking any laws, but also to make sure that we're working with people in the most cooperative, respectful way, to keep us all *out* of court." He nodded as if reinforcing that message, then stepped to the side. "So now I'm going to introduce Riva Singh, the project engineer for this job."

That was maybe their first misstep, Caleb decided. The engineer was beautiful and poised, and when she started speaking, explaining their plans, she sounded like any other Canadian. But her skin was dark, her last name wasn't Dutch or German or British, and for the insular community of Rocky

Creek, that was enough to label her an outsider. A foreigner, regardless of where she was born. There wasn't much open racism in the community, but that didn't mean there wasn't plenty of it under the surface.

But the engineer seemed oblivious to any of those undercurrents. She took Peter Carr's place on the podium and raised a remote control, clicking it until the ceiling-mounted projector sent an image to the screen behind her. A beautiful shot of the fertile farmland they all lived in, looking out toward the lake, and Caleb was pretty sure he knew the exact spot it was taken from in the provincial park. He could see his own property, and he realized again just how close it was to the proposed pit. The engineer was talking, explaining technical details in clear, straightforward terms, but Caleb had trouble paying attention. This was really happening. That was his farm, his home, nestled in right next to the proposed site.

When Singh was done, a few other experts stood up and gave their reports, explaining how the quarry would help the local economy and wouldn't hurt the environment. The slides kept coming, showing graphs and charts, long reports with key phrases highlighted and enlarged to a legible size, and lots of shots of people. Happy engineers in the lab, smiling over positive reports. Happy construction workers in hard hats, operating heavy equipment. Happy families driving happy cars down happy roadways paved with happy aggregates. It was over the top, in Caleb's opinion, but he couldn't deny that the tension in the room had lowered considerably. Happy engineers talking to happy townsfolk, apparently.

Which was more than a little awkward. Caleb glanced sideways and saw Matt's frown, and was reassured. He wasn't the only one who didn't like how things were going. But he wasn't sure there was much Matt could do about any of it, not from the position he was in.

A final slide, and then Peter Carr returned to his place at the podium, smiling out at the audience as if they were all his best friends. "I know that was a lot of information all at once—we've got printed reports for you to take home and read over, and all of this is also available at our website. Like I said, we're committed to being open and honest about this entire process. We're not here to shove the quarry down your throats; we're convinced that once you think about it, you won't really have any objections to it." Another warm smile, and then he said, "So, thank you all for coming. That's the end of our presentation, but we're all planning to stick around for a while, to answer any questions you have, one-on-one. I'll remind you who everyone is: Riva's our project engineer, Malcolm can answer economic questions, and Sean's our ecologist. If you'd just like general questions answered, I'd be happy to help you with that. So, thanks again for coming out, and drive safe."

That was it? They were being dismissed? It made sense, Caleb realized. A full-group question period would give people a chance to hear their neighbors' objections, and could fire the crowd back up to the way it had been before the meeting started. So they were all being managed, just as they'd been managed right through the rest of the presentation. Caleb didn't want to get involved; he wanted to lean back into the shadows and let things flow by him. But he remembered his own words from earlier, the ones Matt had spoken to him years before. It was his town as much as anyone else's, and he had as much responsibility as they did to ensure that it wasn't ruined. And, of course, it was his farm that was right next to the damn pit.

"How many jobs?" he said quickly, his voice loud enough to carry over the rustling of people getting ready to leave. "You said you're bringing jobs to the community, but you didn't give a number. And you didn't say whether they'd be jobs people around here might be able to fill, or whether you'll be bringing in people from outside."

The crowd stilled, but Peter Carr's smile was as warm and relaxed as ever. It was almost overwhelming when he turned it, full force, toward Caleb. "That's a good question. I think Malcolm is going to be setting up over by the windows, there, and I'm sure he can answer that for you."

"It might be a question a lot of people would like to hear the answer to," Caleb forced himself to say. Damn it, everyone was looking at him, and he could feel the heat rising to his face. But it was his town, his farm, so he continued. "You guys are all about efficiency, right? So it'd probably be most efficient to give your answer to the whole group. And you're all about openness, so you wouldn't want to give the impression that you're trying to keep people from hearing something...."

"Of course we aren't," Peter said reassuringly, with another smile. "I just don't want to hold people up. Maybe... why don't we take a short break, to give people who need to be somewhere else a chance to escape, and then we'll see where we are." He nodded toward the crowd, giving them permission to move. The pause was long and a bit awkward, but nobody stirred. Peter's smile still seemed relaxed, but Caleb wondered whether that was all part of the act. "Okay, then. You're all interested in hearing about the jobs. Great. Malcolm, can I pass this over to you?"

"Sure, yeah," Malcolm said, stepping up to the front of the room. "Well, we're not sure about jobs right now, to be honest. We're currently employing about fifty people, with the agricultural operation. The quarry would be more labor intensive— more jobs per acre. So we might lose some of the farming jobs, but we'd have more jobs overall, and we'd absolutely try to hire the farm workers for new jobs in the quarry, assuming they were interested. So, a net increase, for sure." He paused as if hoping he was done, but he read the room well enough to know that he wasn't. "You guys want a number. The problem is—we don't know. The more land we work at once, the more jobs we'll have, but the shorter time the jobs will last. We're still working out plans on that, and I really can't give you a firm number. I don't want to mislead you."

Caleb wasn't sure whether the man was being evasive or honest, but he seemed to be done speaking, and the crowd was apparently going to accept that. Caleb wondered if he had the courage to push any further. He hadn't really cared about the jobs, not for himself; there were other things that concerned him a lot more. It had been his weak attempt to play to the crowd, but it obviously hadn't worked all that well. No big surprise, really; he'd half expected some of them to storm out of the place in protest for him daring to open his mouth. But there were questions that needed to be asked, and people needed to hear the answers. Caleb took a deep breath.

But he didn't have to speak again. "What about the water?" It was Mr. Shackleton, the geography teacher. "You're planning to go a long way below the water table, right? And the quarrying will produce a lot of silt, and there will be fuel and oil and whatever else introduced into the runoff. We're upstream from an internationally recognized bird sanctuary, and the wetlands there are crucial to a number of species. You said you were confident that the water could be cleaned. I don't share your confidence."

This time, the pause was only awkward for the Caplan representatives. The community members were getting their energy back, the indignation that had brought them to the meeting returning, and they swiveled back to face the front of the room, waiting for an answer.

The ecologist was the logical one to answer, but he kept his back turned to the audience, even when Peter Carr leaned over and nudged him. Finally, it was Carr who stood up. "I'm sorry to hear that you're not confident. That's something that worries me... it's absolutely our goal to have you all feel comfortable with the process."

"Let's stop worrying about 'the process' and start worrying about the facts." It was Carol Diefenbaker speaking. She and her husband worked one of the farms right next to the proposed quarry land. The back of their property lined up with the back of Caleb's, and he knew her well. Well enough to know that she was a pit bull; she didn't look for trouble, but if it found her, she bit down hard and didn't let go. The Caplan folks had better brace themselves. Caleb smiled, and saw Matt grinning beside him. "It's great that you want us to be confident and comfortable, but that doesn't count for much if we're confident and comfortable in the wrong damn things! I want to know that my well is safe, and I want to be able to enjoy my property without worrying about shaking and dust and noise coming from next door! I want to be able to drive down the road without having to deal with hundreds of gravel trucks. Hundreds, that's what I heard! And, yeah, I want to know about the jobs, and the wetlands, and all the rest of it. You've given us a lot of nicely polished *bullshit* tonight, and if you're getting out of the farming business, then you really don't need any of that for fertilizer!"

"Yeah!"

Caleb couldn't tell who said it first, but it was soon followed by whooping and agreement and applause, and the crowd that had been about to file away and go home was suddenly alive, involved, and angry. Just like they damn well should be. It was *their* town too, and they shouldn't let some slick talker from the city pull the wool over their eyes. It didn't matter that the man was beautiful, not if he was using his looks to do ugly things.

Caleb smiled in triumph and looked toward the front of the room to see the beautiful man staring back at him. His expression was strange. He didn't seem angry, and he certainly didn't look intimidated. He was absorbing the noise of the room as if they were cheering for him, and he was looking at Caleb with what really seemed to be gratitude. He was *glad* that Caleb had spoken up, happy that all of this was happening. But Caleb had no idea why.

CHAPTER TWO

"YOU are an arrogant son of a bitch, Carr." Riva Singh shook her head in familiar exasperation. "You're *happy* things blew up like that, aren't you? Just so you'd have a bigger challenge to fix?"

Peter shrugged. "I'm happy, yeah. But it's not about the challenge, not really. It's just—it's nice to see the system working, you know?"

"How the hell was that 'the system working'? That was the system getting all screwed up by a bunch of redneck locals who can't just go along with the damn plan." Riva was sitting in the passenger seat as Peter drove the company sedan. It was just as well that she wasn't driving, because she was pretty worked up.

Peter smiled, but he was careful to keep his face turned forward—focusing his attention on the dark country road, and also preventing Riva from seeing his expression. They'd had this conversation before, and they'd probably have it again. They were the troubleshooting team for a multinational corporation that tended toward ambitious, controversial projects. They worked well together and were good friends, but that didn't mean they agreed on much... including the value of democratic debate. "It's the adversarial system. They give their best arguments, we give ours, and we find the truth somewhere in the middle. We find the best path. I mean... the company needs to know that people have their eyes on it, right? We wouldn't bother with all the environmental stuff, all the community-building, if we didn't have to. And we wouldn't have to if we didn't know that people were going to be attacking us every time we try to build something new. We're all playing our parts." Just because they'd had the argument before didn't mean Peter couldn't still sound passionate about it all. He threw in a charming, earnest smile for good measure, but Riva had known him long enough to be immune.

"No. *My* part is overseeing a project. *My* part is making sure that things are built as efficiently as possible, on time and on budget, without interference or complication. That's *my* part."

"Yup." Peter refused to be bothered. Partly because he knew that was what would aggravate Riva the most, but it was also his natural disposition. Life was interesting, but it wasn't something to get upset about. Things would happen as they would, and he would make sure everything worked out, one way or the other. That was his strength, and he took advantage of it whenever he could. "That's your part. And their part is stirring up a fuss and scrutinizing everything we do and keeping us honest."

"And your part? Does your part mostly involve sitting back and laughing at all of us?"

"I wouldn't say 'mostly,' no." Peter grinned as he pulled the car into the parking spot in front of Riva's motel room. "It's a minor aspect of the job. But it *is* my favorite."

"It's all just a game, huh?" Riva's voice was more serious than Peter had anticipated, and he turned to look at her. Her face was lit by the motel's exterior lights, and he could see her eyes, big and brown, turned toward him.

"What's up, Riva?" He was tired, but Riva was a friend, and he made sure his tone was gentle. "I mean, is there something going on that you want to talk about?" He was happy to hear what she had to say, but if she didn't want to discuss it, that was fine too. They were friends, but that didn't mean there were no boundaries.

But, as usual, Riva was ready to share. She sighed and dramatically flopped back against the leather seats. "Do you ever get tired of it? Traveling all over the place, staying in dumps like this, turning people's lives upside down?"

"Are *you* tired of it?" He shifted in his seat so he could face her more easily. "Or are you just tired, all round? You've been putting in a lot of hours the last couple weeks...."

"Scott asked me to marry him," she said softly.

It caught Peter off guard, and he took a moment to think about it. "He's not living in the fifties. He doesn't expect you to quit your job and stay home and cook and clean for him."

"No, of course not. It's just... I think maybe I want to. Not the cooking and cleaning—you know me better than that! But maybe I want to settle down. Stop traveling so much." Her expression was almost pleading, as if it was really important to her that he understand. "I could find a job at the home office, probably, or if they can't find something for me, I could find another firm. I just... is this all there is, Pete? Just... this?"

"This?" He looked through the windshield at the dingy motel. "This is the best place that's close to the site. We usually stay at better hotels." He was pretty sure she was looking for something deeper, but he really had no idea what to say on any of the more fundamental issues. He was good at thinking on his feet, but somehow this sentiment from Riva had knocked him off balance.

Her disappointed look hurt. He deserved it, but he still hated it. And he hated it even more when she forced a cheerful smile onto her face and pulled the car door open. "Right. Well, my gray sheets and lumpy mattress are calling to me. Breakfast meeting at seven thirty tomorrow?" The rest of the presentation team had just come in for the town meeting, but Peter and Riva were on-site for the full battle.

"Sure," Peter agreed. He sat there for a moment as she climbed out of the car, then hurriedly pulled his own door open and got out. "Riva?"

She turned and waited.

"I don't understand. Not yet. But I'm going to try to, okay?" He waited for her half smile, then added, "And congratulations. On the wedding. I mean—I assume you said 'yes'?"

She nodded. "I did."

"Okay, then. Congratulations. And say the same to Scott. He's a lucky man." He grinned to show her that he meant it. "Sleep tight."

Riva still didn't look totally satisfied, but she managed a smile as she said, "You too. See you in the morning."

She stepped inside her room and closed the door behind her, and Peter headed for his own room two doors down. Riva was right; the motel was a dive. But that wasn't something Peter worried about. And it wasn't something Riva would normally worry about, either.

He pulled his jacket off and hung it carefully in the closet, then did the same with his belt and pants. His tie and shirt followed, and then he wandered into the bathroom wearing only his socks and underwear. He leaned over the chipped basin and stared at himself in the mirror. *Is this all there is?* What the hell did that mean?

It wasn't like he worked *all* the time. Well, according to Marty he did, but Marty had been looking for an excuse to break up for months. He'd said Peter cared more about his job than he did about anybody or anything else, but... that was natural, surely. His job was important, and he was damned good at it. And Marty had never had a problem with spending the money Peter earned from working long hours.

Is this all there is? He looked in the mirror and made a face at himself, then turned in the general direction of Riva's room and made a face at her, as well. They had a job to do, a quarry to promote, and all this soul-searching wasn't going to get the townsfolk on board and the excavation started.

He brushed his teeth and headed back to the main room. He had some reading that needed to be attended to, and some e-mails to answer, and then he'd get a good night's sleep and deal with Riva in the morning. He'd deal with the town in the morning too. Everything was going to work out just fine, he decided as he settled into the scratchy sheets over the lumpy mattress. It was all part of the process.

CHAPTER THREE

THE diner was always busy at breakfast time, but it seemed especially crowded the morning after the town hall meeting. Caleb usually sat at the counter when he came in alone, but there were no stools available. He was thinking about ordering something he could eat in the car when Becky, the owner's daughter, frowned in his direction.

"You on your own, Caleb? Mind if we stick you at a table with some other folks?"

Caleb was fine with it, but he couldn't guarantee the others would be. His stomach tightened a little, but he wouldn't back down. If the other people were homophobic assholes, that was their problem. "Yeah, sure," he said, trying to sound relaxed and confident.

"Great." Becky was seventeen, maybe five feet tall if she stretched, and she carried herself with the easy authority and purpose of a four-star general. She was totally comfortable as she turned to the couple ahead of Caleb in line. "There's only two of you, right? Mind some company?"

Caleb saw the man's nod of acquiescence and tried to figure out why the couple's backs looked familiar, but then he got distracted. He didn't want to be as paranoid as Matt accused him of being, but as Becky led the three of them through the crowded restaurant, it really felt like quite a few people were sending dirty looks in his direction. What, it was okay for the fag to eat at the counter, but he'd better not mix with the wholesome people at the tables? Were people really that closed-minded?

They reached the table, which Becky wiped with a quick and efficient swipe of her rag, and when the other two people turned to take their seats, Caleb realized the dirty looks hadn't been directed at him. Or, if they had, they had been for consorting with the enemy, not for consorting with same-sex partners.

"Peter Carr," the beautiful man from the night before said as he extended his hand. "And this is Riva Singh. You were at the meeting last night, right? Asked the first question?"

Caleb managed to reach his hand out for the obligatory shake, but he really didn't think he was going to be able to get any words out past the constriction in his throat. He honestly couldn't say whether he was more worried about being seen with the people who were trying to ruin his farm and the entire town, or about trying to eat a meal with the most gorgeous man on the planet. Damn it.

The other two exchanged a barely perceptible glance, then sat down. They were apparently willing to overlook the shy bumbling of a local yokel. "Yes," Caleb blurted out. It was far too late; the others probably couldn't even remember what question he was answering. He thought about leaving. The table, the diner, the town, possibly the country. But he would call even *more* attention to himself if he didn't sit down, so he jerked a chair out and sank into it quickly. "The first question," he echoed, even later than his earlier incoherence.

"Thanks for that," Carr said with an easy smile. "It was good to get the discussion started."

"It didn't seem like you *wanted* any discussion." Caleb honestly wasn't sure where those words had come from. Probably the same mysterious pit that had produced the original question the day before. He busied himself with adding milk and sugar to the coffee Becky was pouring for him.

"No, it's good. Discussion is a bit messy, sometimes, but...

you know. Lots of good things are messy." Carr nodded as if he was agreeing with Caleb. "People need to know what's going on. They need the whole picture. I understand that."

"And what if they get the whole picture and don't like it? What if more information makes them even more worried about the quarry?" Caleb had forgotten his coffee, at least for the moment.

"I'm sorry, I didn't get your name...."

Of course not. Giving a name would have been something a normal person would have done. "I'm Caleb. Sinclair. Caleb Sinclair." Caleb took a sip from his cup before he started babbling about his middle name, or the names of his dogs, or whatever other nonsense might come out of his addled brain.

"Caleb, hi." A brief, dazzling smile, and then the man was right back into his speech. "You were there last night, Caleb. Do you really think it's possible for people to be more dead set against a project than the crowd was at the start of the meeting? I really think anything we do here can only improve the situation." But then the broad, smooth brow furrowed into a slight frown, and Carr looked over at his partner as if for confirmation. "Caleb Sinclair... we sent you a letter, right? I was going to be giving you a call in the next couple days to see if we could set up a meeting."

"A meeting? I mean, I got a letter, yeah. Saying what you were planning to do. But what's the meeting for?"

"You own one of the properties right next door to the proposed site, don't you? Adjacent to the Dean farm?"

"I don't think they really want it called the Dean farm anymore," Caleb objected. "Not when you're about to turn it into a huge hole in the ground."

"Oh, okay. Sorry. But that's where you live? That's why we wanted to set up a meeting—you're one of our closest neighbors, and we wanted to make sure you had all the information you need."

"You keep talking about information as if it's going to solve everything!" Caleb caught himself. He had no idea where this wave of audacity was coming from, but he didn't think the entire diner needed to hear his concerns. He tried to modulate the volume as he said, "If you dig as deep as you're planning and my well goes dry or gets contaminated, all the information in the world isn't going to help me out. If the wildlife is scared away by the noise, I don't need 'information' to tell me about it. If the blasting makes my cows' milk dry up, you can't *inform* them back into being productive."

"You're a dairy farmer? I didn't think we had any dairy farms that close." Another look at Riva, this time vaguely accusatory, as if she had been withholding information.

Caleb didn't like having to defend the woman's research, but he wasn't going to lie. "No, not dairy. I run a few head of beef, that's all. But that's not the point. The point is, if your information tells me that your quarry is going to mess up my farm, I'm not going to be happy. And if it tells me that it's *not* going to mess up my farm... I won't believe it. So I don't think information is going to be all that useful."

Carr nodded slowly and then took a thoughtful sip of his coffee. It was impossible to tell whether he was sincerely thinking things over, or whether it was all an act. Finally, he said, "We can take baseline measurements. Or you could hire the people to do it, and we could pay for them. Flow and quality of your well water, wildlife populations, noise or lack thereof. And then, if the quarry *does* affect you negatively, you'd have evidence to prove it. We could compensate you accordingly. I mean, I don't think those things are going to happen. But if they do—you'd be compensated."

"Compensated?" Caleb hadn't planned to do it, but he suddenly found himself rising to his feet. "Compensated? For the destruction of a farm that's been in my family for five generations? How could you possibly compensate me for that?" He'd managed to keep his voice at a reasonable level, at least, but it hadn't really done him any good. The diner's patrons had already been monitoring his table pretty closely, and when he stood up, all other conversation had stopped completely. Everyone had heard what he'd said, and for a change, the attention sent in his direction seemed generally positive. But he didn't find it much more enjoyable than the negative regard had been. He just wanted to blur into the background and be left alone.

The whole thing was too much. The beautiful man was still looking at him as if he was hoping the conversation would continue, the diner's patrons were staring, and Becky just wanted him to sit down and get out of her way so she could get her breakfast specials delivered. "I have to go," Caleb said as calmly as he could, and he spun around and headed for the door. He didn't look behind him, didn't even slow down until he was safely out of the diner and behind the wheel of his pickup. He shut the door, took a deep breath, and swore softly. He was a mess, and he had enough on his plate without worrying about the opinion of some handsome stranger from the city.

He needed to put it out of his mind. The town was used to his awkwardness and would forget about his outburst soon enough, and Peter Carr had probably already dismissed him as some sort of crackpot. That was just as well. He shifted the truck into gear and pulled out of the parking lot. He had work to do, things he was good at, and he needed to focus on them. He needed to stop thinking about people staring at him, and about beautiful smiles that could never really be for him.

Chapter Four

Peter watched the pickup pulling out of the parking lot. "He didn't get any breakfast."

"I don't think that's number one on his list of worries." Riva sipped her coffee and watched Peter. He felt like a specimen in a laboratory.

"I didn't—I wasn't out of line, was I? I mean, he had a good point about the compensation. That was something we could have talked about. He could have advanced a strong argument on that front."

"Not everyone's like you, Peter." Riva frowned, then added, "Thank God. Most people don't look at their lives as 'advancing arguments.' Most people have genuine emotions."

"I have genuine emotions!"

"Curiosity is not an emotion." Riva stopped talking as the waitress returned, and it was just as well. Peter hadn't really liked what she was saying. It sounded like more of her *is this all there is* nonsense, and he was just getting that out of his head. He didn't need another dose of it. It was confusing, and there was no point to it.

"Breakfast special, please," Riva told the waitress. "Scrambled eggs, wheat toast, and bacon."

But the waitress wasn't writing anything down. Maybe she just had a good memory, but Peter didn't think so. He was pretty sure she'd been using her pad to record the orders from the other customers. "Is everything okay?" He made sure that he sounded concerned, not confrontational.

"What happened with Caleb?" The girl frowned as if she already knew more of the answer than she wanted.

"Oh. I guess... I wasn't as tactful as I should have been. We were talking business, and... I said the wrong thing. He got upset."

The waitress didn't look impressed, and Peter wondered whether she and Sinclair had some sort of relationship. They hadn't seemed especially close when she'd shown them all to the table, but she was taking the whole thing pretty seriously. It was beginning to look like maybe Sinclair wasn't going to be the only person who left the diner hungry that morning. But the girl finally lifted her pencil to her notepad and looked at Riva, saying, "Scrambled, wheat, and bacon, right?"

"That's right," Riva confirmed. "Thanks."

"And you?" The waitress's eyebrow lifted, as if she was daring Peter to cross her.

"The same, please. Thanks."

The waitress turned toward the kitchen, and Riva said, "Since when do you like your eggs scrambled?"

"Since I was afraid the waitress would kick me out if I said more than a few words." Peter huffed out a sigh of relief that was only a little bit exaggerated. "Damn. Sinclair's got some friends in this town."

"Or you've got some enemies."

"Me? Shouldn't that be *we* have some enemies?"

"I'm just the loyal brown servant, sahib. You're the big white man, the one they all look at and hate."

"Yeah, great. Is that the excuse you're going to use when they come for us with the torches?"

"Come for *you* with the torches." Riva smiled peacefully and sipped her coffee. It gave Peter a moment to think.

"He was standing next to the Deans' son last night. The doctor." Peter had noticed the two men entering together even before Sinclair had spoken up. They'd looked like a couple, at first, and Peter had wondered how that worked in a small, conservative town. But he'd recognized Matt Dean pretty quickly, and knowing that the doctor was married, had adjusted his perception. "They must have grown up together, living next door like that."

"You're back on Caleb Sinclair? Yeah, I guess they probably know each other."

"The Deans have been taking some heat. Well, the parents are down in Florida, I guess. But I've heard people slamming them."

"Well, people have a point." Riva looked at Peter with a challenging expression. "You really think we would have gone ahead with this project if we hadn't gotten their land? Almost two thousand acres, all in one parcel... we'd have had a hell of a time putting that together ourselves, picking up individual farms here and there."

"Yeah, sure. But, what? They weren't supposed to sell their farm, ever? The boy's a doctor, the girl's married and living in Australia or something... the parents could never retire?"

"Of course they could. They did. They sold their farm, and now we're putting a quarry in." Riva frowned at him. "Where are you coming from with all this?"

"I don't know." That was true. He really didn't, and it was bugging him. "It just doesn't seem right. People were giving the *son* dirty looks last night. I mean... what was he supposed to do about any of it?"

"People are angry—that's your problem? What about being part of the process, and it's all just a good way to make sure we find the best balance of interests?" Her confused frown faded into an understanding grin. "Oh. Wait. It's okay for people to be mad at *you*. *That's* part of the process. You just don't like it when they're mad at *each other*. Is that it?"

"Maybe." Peter wasn't sorry that the waitress arrived then with their breakfasts. It was nice to have a way to distract Riva from insisting on a better answer to her question. Peter liked playing psychologist with other people, but he really didn't feel like being analyzed himself.

By the time their food was served the conversation had moved on, and they spent the rest of their meal planning the day's tasks. As Peter had told Sinclair, the plan was to visit each of the neighbors, to introduce themselves and offer any information that might be needed or hear any opinions that might be offered. It wasn't strictly necessary; the quarry didn't need the neighbors' permission to move forward. But things went more smoothly if everyone got along, and besides, Peter liked the challenge of it all.

They were just finishing their second cups of coffee when a new arrival came and stood at their table, looking at them expectantly. He looked vaguely familiar, his compact body carried in a way that resonated somehow in Peter's memory banks. Peter tried to figure out the resemblance but had no luck. "Can I help you with something?" he finally asked.

"You're the quarry people," the man said. There was no hint of a question in his voice, but he seemed to be waiting for a response anyway.

"We're with Caplan International," Peter agreed. He stood up and extended his hand. "I'm Peter Carr." Some protective instinct made him reluctant to introduce Riva. It was probably a breach of business etiquette, but Peter would just have to hope Riva didn't mind.

"Trevor Sinclair," the stranger said, shaking Peter's hand. The last name made Peter realize who the man reminded him off. The resemblance wasn't strong, but it was there. The same sandy hair, the same fine-boned face, but a totally different impression, somehow. Maybe it was the eyes; Trevor's were a mid-brown, light and quick, while Caleb's were deep and dark. "I own the farm next to the Dean place." Trevor didn't wait for an invitation, just pulled out a chair and sank into it. "I thought we should talk."

"You own... there's only one name on the title to the Sinclair property," Peter said carefully.

"It's a family farm. It's half mine."

"Okay." There was no reason to argue it. Maybe the guy was right—and even if he wasn't, it was none of Peter's business. "So, do you have any questions about the quarry? Anything you'd like to discuss?"

"Yeah, absolutely." Trevor leaned forward and braced his forearms against the side of the table. "I'd like to talk about selling the place to you."

"Selling it? We... we've already made an offer to the registered owner, but it was refused. We've gone ahead with plans based on the current properties we own."

"Yeah, fine, but you have to leave a buffer, right? That's what I heard you said at the meeting last night. So if you owned the farm, *it* could be the buffer and you could dig the quarry out further, even if you didn't go right into our land. You could change the plans, and get a lot more gravel. That could mean big bucks, but it won't be easy. I mean... my brother's a pain in the ass. He seems quiet, but when he gets something in his head, he's really stubborn."

"Yes, I think we've seen a hint of that already. But he's not interested in selling; as I said, we already made an offer."

"That was before he knew about the quarry, right? When you first came to town, you were just buying farms; nobody knew what it was for."

"Okay...."

"So now the property would be worth less to him. Because it's going to be all loud, or whatever. But it's still worth the same to you, because you're just going to use it as a buffer. So, I think you should make us another offer."

It wasn't a terrible idea. The company had certainly made similar purchases in the past, but not as a first option. The original offer to purchase Sinclair's property had been based on one configuration of the quarry, and when the man had refused to sell, the company had gone with another layout. So the Sinclair property was no longer really needed, and there were only two reasons they'd buy it. One reason would be to shut up a strong opponent of the project. Peter remembered Caleb Sinclair's quiet outrage, and the way his eyes had shone with the passion of someone who truly believed in what he was saying. Yeah, he could turn into a problem, if Peter allowed it.

The other reason the company might buy, of course, was if purchasing the property was part of a settlement reached after the quarry started working. If the quarry *did* make things unliveable next door, the company could buy the residents out as part of a compensation package. But those packages tended to be expensive, and it was generally cheaper and tidier to take care of things before such steps became necessary. So the brother could definitely be useful. But there was something about him that Peter just didn't trust.

"I don't think we're at that stage yet," he told Trevor. "But we'd certainly like to keep the lines of communication open. I wouldn't want to rule out the possibility."

"And you'll keep me in the loop?" Trevor seemed to have lost the somewhat antagonistic air he'd had when he first approached. They were all friends now, apparently. "My brother can be... he's pretty emotional, sometimes. He doesn't always see the smart thing to do. But I can handle him. So it's probably best if I'm your contact person, and then I'll make sure he understands the situation." Trevor leaned forward a little, as if he was about to share a secret. No, Peter realized, it wasn't a secret; it was an offer, and Peter was supposed to think it was too good to pass up. "Actually, I'm between projects right now, and from what I've seen, I may be able to help you out with this whole thing. You're smooth; I'll give you that, but you're an outsider, and people here are never really going to trust you." He smiled again. "I was born and raised here. Play hockey with half the town, get drunk with the other half. Well, I get drunk with the hockey players too, I guess! So I could be really helpful for you—a sort of agent."

Peter wasn't quite sure what he was dealing with. The man was charming, in a superficial way, and again, his suggestion wasn't outrageous. But Peter didn't know enough about him, not by a long shot. "That's absolutely another thing for me to keep in mind," he said. "I appreciate the offer. Are you working somewhere else, right now, or are you pretty flexible?"

"I'm flexible," Trevor said. "I've got things coming up, of course, but I'm my own boss. I make my own schedule."

Peter refused to look at Riva; he didn't need to see her smirk to know how she'd interpret Trevor's statement. And she was probably right. The guy was probably unemployed and shiftless. But he was a local, and as such, he was one of the people Peter was supposed to be persuading. So he smiled, and raised a hand to get the waitress's attention. "A cup of coffee?" he offered to Trevor.

"Sounds good," the man agreed. He leaned back in his chair again, and his smile was positively smug. Obviously everything was going the way he had planned. Peter just hoped the satisfaction wouldn't turn to bitterness if Peter stopped going along with the plans.

CHAPTER FIVE

CALEB spent the day in London. It was the closest city of any size, and the biggest market for his custom cabinetry. His current project was challenging—the Daughtreys had a *very* specific vision for their new den, but they didn't really have the words to translate that concept into instructions. So Caleb was spending a lot of time sketching, working out drawings on his computer, and groaning in frustration. But at least the clients were willing to pay for all that time. And he was driving home with a folder full of marked-up drawings and the clients' appreciation and admiration still on replay in his head, so he wasn't going to complain.

There wasn't ever much about his job that he'd complain about, really. He did good work and paid attention to the right details, and he had clients lined up until mid-fall. And he'd been having good luck with sales of his individual pieces too. It was one of the few areas of his life where he felt confident. His skills were portable, he supposed; if the quarry went through and made his life miserable, he could pick up and relocate. He could find somewhere with a bigger market and more rich people. But, damn it! He'd stuck around when the town decided to shun him, held his ground when they spray-painted *Faggot* on the side of his pickup... he wasn't going to run away now.

He tried not to look in at the Dean property as he drove past it. The fields looked much as they had in the fall; corn stubble in one, another bare earth waiting for the plow, and more that he couldn't see. It was impossible to imagine them gone, replaced by a gaping hole. And hard to imagine the quiet country road he was turned into a thoroughfare for hundreds of gravel trucks a day. He wondered what the time frame on the project was; maybe that, at least, would be useful information to get from Peter Carr.

The road rose to follow one of the area's few hills, and the trees became thicker and taller. Caleb stopped at his mailbox and barely glanced at the envelopes he extracted, then continued down his long, winding driveway. He recognized the car parked in front of the house, and wasn't surprised when Diesel and Diego came, barking, to greet him. Matt knew where the Hide-a-Key was and he wouldn't come to visit without letting the dogs out.

"Hey, beasts," Caleb said as he opened the door of the truck. It was a bit tricky finding room for his feet with eight dancing paws in the way, but he managed, and reached a hand out in greeting. The dogs were brothers, two of six mastiff-type puppies that some asshole had left in a cardboard box down at the roadside a couple of years before. Caleb had never thought of himself as a dog person, and he'd fully intended to hold onto the puppies just long enough to find them homes. But somehow these two—Diesel full of bravado and self-importance, Diego shyer and sweeter—had worked their way into his heart. He'd placed the others from the litter with good, caring owners, but had never really tried to get rid of these two. "Were you good dogs today?" He headed toward the front porch with the dogs bounding around him in celebration of his homecoming. "Did you offer Uncle Matt a beer?"

"They did," Matt confirmed from his Adirondack chair by the front door. He lifted a half-emptied green bottle in evidence.

"Good boys." Caleb reached for the door handle. "I'm going to get my own, since apparently the beasts only serve guests. You want another?"

"Yeah," Matt said, and he took a long pull from the bottle in his hand.

Caleb headed inside, the dogs trailing behind him. Matt wasn't usually much of a drinker. And it was just past five o'clock on a weeknight; Matt would usually be at work, or home with his wife. Caleb's stomach tightened a little, but he forced himself to relax. Maybe Matt was just starting a new tradition. Maybe Sarah was working late. She taught elementary school, and her hours were usually pretty regular except at report card time, but maybe she had a meeting or something. There was nothing to get tense about.

Still, Caleb knew something was off. He headed back to the porch and handed one of the beers to Matt, then sank into the second Adirondack chair. The air was cool but they were both wearing warm jackets, and it was nice to be outside after a long winter stuck indoors. Diego sank down into a compact ball right next to Caleb's feet, while Diesel sat more warily just at the top of the stairs, ready to bound off and dispose of any threats. Both dogs were about the same size, tipping the vet's scales at over a hundred pounds each, but Diego always made himself seem much, much smaller. Caleb could sympathize with the impulse, but he was glad that Diesel was around to remind the rest of them to be brave.

Nobody spoke for a while. Finally, Matt said, "I had four patients who didn't show up today. No call, no explanation. They just didn't come."

Caleb didn't think he needed to ask why. "Their loss, man. I mean, there's a serious doctor shortage. Blackball those assholes and fill your schedule with people who aren't going to be petty bitches about stuff."

"Carol Diefenbaker was one of them." Matt stared at his beer bottle. "We used to swim in her pond, remember? She'd let us have campfires there, and cookouts…. She's not an asshole, Caleb."

"Bill Taylor used to let my mom run a tab at the grocery store when we were short on cash. Then after I came out, he told his kids to stop hanging out with me." Caleb wasn't quite sure what the point of that little story was. "There aren't that many people who are pure asshole, all the way through. That doesn't mean it's okay for them to pull that shit."

"Mrs. Diefenbaker was friends with my mom."

"So maybe she feels betrayed, or something. By your *mom*. Not by you."

"Is that how you feel? That my parents let you down, but *I'm* okay?" Matt shook his head. "You're going to get just as burned by this, if the quarry goes through. You've got as much to lose as anybody—more than most of them. But you're not even a little pissed?"

"I made a big scene and stormed out of the diner this morning, trying to get away from that company lawyer. Had to drive through McDonalds up in the city just so I wouldn't starve to death." That was maybe a little dramatic, but Caleb was well aware of Dr. Matt's views on fast food, and didn't need a lecture. "I'm plenty pissed. But not at you. Or your parents. I mean, they thought they were selling to ginseng farmers, right? But even if they'd known... they have a right to retire, Matt. It was *their* land." Caleb had been thinking about this for a while, and he was pretty sure he was right. "The same people around here who were putting up the 'It's our land, government, back off' signs a couple years ago? They're the ones who are bitching loudest about this now. Suddenly, they're all *about* community and everyone having a say in what other people do on their own property."

Matt's smile was real, but sad. "Yeah. And they're the people who aren't getting medical care they need, because they can't stand to be in the same room with me." Diego had been listening to the conversation, his eyes always on the person speaking, and now he stood up and walked the few steps until he was able to sit next to Matt and lay his head on the man's knee. Matt smiled at him and reached a hand out to fondle his ears.

Caleb wished he could offer comfort as easily. "They'll get over it. Or they'll drag their asses up to the city and find a doctor up there. You can't take responsibility for everything, man."

"I'm supposed to take responsibility for my patients, though." Matt stared gloomily out toward the forest's edge. He was silent for quite a while before adding, "And I'm supposed to take responsibility for my wife."

Caleb waited for that to make sense, but nothing came to him, and finally Matt said, "Sarah's pregnant again. Seven weeks." He didn't sound excited by the news.

"Shit." Well, no, that wasn't right. "I mean—congratulations. Just... how's it going, so far?"

"Fine." Matt made the word sound like a curse. "Just like it went all the other times. Everything's good until just before the end of the first trimester, right when we're finally thinking that maybe this time we're going to make it...." Matt finished his beer with a defiant gulp, and for a moment Caleb was pretty sure his friend was going to hurl the bottle over to smash against a tree trunk. But Matt sighed and set the bottle down on the deck with enough care to make it clear that the effort was conscious. "I didn't want her to try again. I begged her not to. I said we could adopt. I said we'd be good for a kid with special needs, even—we're educated, financially and emotionally stable—but she...."

"She wants this," Caleb said. "She wants to be pregnant." He didn't know if it would make things better or worse, but he added, "She loves you so much. And she's got it in her head that it's her job to give you this."

"And it's my job to keep her safe. I'm a fucking doctor, Caleb. I spent almost a decade learning about the human body, figuring out how to help people. And I can't do a damn thing for my own damn wife."

"Nothing? I mean, you've been to the specialist, right? He said... last time, you were talking about bed rest, how that might help. If it would—I can help out, man. My work is flexible. I can drop in on her during the day, if she needs. Whatever."

"Yeah, thanks." Matt's voice was dead. "But the specialist... he put that out there, like, as a way to give us something constructive to do, but he said it won't really help. He said...." There was a crack in Matt's voice, and he took a deep breath before continuing. "He said that the most important thing was keeping calm, and not worrying about anything." His snort was half laughter, half disgust. "As if that's fucking possible, when's she's sitting around waiting for her fifth fucking miscarriage." A pause, and then he said, "As if it's possible, when the whole town has turned against her and her husband. I talked her into moving down here, Caleb. She wanted to stay in the city, but she gave in when she saw how important this was to me. I brought her here. It's my fault."

"She loves it here, Matt. You know that. She's glad you guys moved down." But that was the easy part. "And the whole town hasn't turned against you. Four people didn't show up today. You probably had, what, twenty or thirty appointments? Most of them came."

"Four didn't come and didn't call. Five more called with excuses."

"A couple of those were probably real. Something just came up. But even if all nine of them cancelled because of the quarry— okay, A is for assholes. And B is for bullshit. They're being pissy, but they aren't going to stay away long-term. Doctor shortage, remember?"

"It's their bodies, Caleb. They have a right to see a doctor they don't hate. I don't want patients who just couldn't get in anywhere else. I want them to come to me because they trust me."

"And twenty or so people did that, today. Right?"

"Yeah." But Matt didn't sound convinced. "Sarah... she doesn't seem aware of it, yet. She's been sticking around the house, mostly. Just sitting there, afraid to move and jar the baby loose, or something. She took a couple days off work, even." Matt shook his head angrily and looked out at the forest. "What am I supposed to do, Caleb? She's not supposed to have any stress! So I can't really tell her about this. But I don't want someone to say something to her, and for her to have had no warning. I don't... Jesus, Caleb, I have no idea what I'm supposed to do."

"She's your wife, Matt. She loves you and you guys are good together. And she's not stupid, *and* you're a terrible liar. She's going to know something's up, and if you don't tell her what it is, she's going to assume it's her and the baby." The rest of it, Caleb wasn't sure about, but this seemed crystal clear. "Talk to her. It'll be more stressful for her to have her husband lying to her than to hear that a few people are being pissy bitches."

Matt frowned at him. "You're all Mr. Logical now. But how did it feel when they were all against you? I seem to remember you being pretty damn upset about it."

"Yeah, and I survived. You talked me down. It's our town too—remember?"

Matt didn't answer for a while. Then he stood up with a burst of decisive energy, making Diego scurry to his feet in alarm. Matt ignored him. "Okay, yeah. Fuck it. I gotta go talk to my wife."

"Yeah, you do!" Caleb said. He tried to sound enthusiastic without coming across as demented. It wasn't easy. "It'll be good, you'll see."

The look Matt gave him suggested that the not-demented part of the plan hadn't worked too well, but Matt was an old friend and he let it go. "Okay. Thanks for the beer and the ear."

"And the valuable advice. Don't forget about that."

"Yeah, okay. Thanks for that too." Matt bent to grip Diego's ruff in both hands, giving him a quick but thorough massage. "Good dog, Diego. If you ever get tired of all the nonsense out here, you can come live with me."

"No, he can't," Caleb corrected. "Get your own dog."

"Too bad you want to stand in the way of true love, Caleb. This dog is obviously crazy about me." But Diego pulled himself away from Matt's hands just as Diesel let out a growling bark and bounded down the porch steps, Diego close behind him.

Caleb didn't recognize the car coming up his driveway, and apparently Matt didn't, either, since he stood there and waited along with Caleb. They both saw the driver at about the same time.

"Son of a bitch," Matt said. "What the hell is *he* doing here?"

They watched as Peter Carr guided his sedan in beside Matt's. "He said he wanted to set up a meeting," Caleb said. "To give me information."

"Information? What the hell use is that going to be?"

"Yeah, that's about what I said when he mentioned it. Right before I stormed out of the diner."

"Giving you an excuse to eat an artery-clogging fast-food breakfast," Matt said, raising an eyebrow. "Did you think you were going to sneak that past me?"

"You're not the boss of me, man." Caleb jutted his jaw out, hoping to earn a grin, but he was disappointed.

"No, I guess not. You can eat whatever crap you want." Matt frowned toward the driveway. The lawyer was still in his car, and the dogs had positioned themselves just outside the driver's door, Diesel growling ferociously, Diego looking unsure but willing to follow his brother's lead. "You want me to stick around?"

A significant part of Caleb wanted exactly that, but he didn't need to add to Matt's worries. "Nah, it's fine. Me and the beasts can take care of him."

"You're sure?"

"Yeah." Matt started walking toward the driveway, and Caleb fell in behind him. "Diesel, sit," he ordered, and the dog gave him a reluctant look before obeying. He was still growling, though, and Caleb didn't ask him to stop. Keeping the lawyer cowering in his car felt pretty good. Caleb turned his attention to Matt. "You're going to be fine. You *and* Sarah. Say 'hi' to her for me, okay?"

"Yeah, I will." Matt looked like he maybe had a bit more to say, but he glanced toward the man in the car and shook his head. "Crazy times, huh? Call me if you need backup."

"Go home," Caleb ordered, and Matt nodded, then climbed into his car. Diesel was still growling, but the lawyer had opened the car door anyway, and stuck one cautious foot out to rest on the ground. Two dogs that looked like Rottweilers crossed with grizzly bears, and the guy was coming out to meet them. He was either stupid, or... or what? Caleb had no idea what the other option was, and it was a bit unnerving. Because whatever other impressions he had of the lawyer's character, stupidity was pretty much out of the question.

CHAPTER SIX

IT ALL came down to confidence. At least, Peter sincerely hoped it did. He shifted his weight onto the foot outside the car door, moving slowly but not hesitantly, and raised himself out of the seat. "Hey, guys," he said to the dogs, and then he ignored them and looked over toward Caleb. Hopefully the man had his animals under some degree of control. And hopefully Peter was right that they wouldn't attack if he didn't look like prey or a threat, or if they weren't ordered to. And, Peter realized, hopefully Caleb wouldn't give that order.

"I hope I'm not intruding; you didn't respond to my message, but I was out at the site, and I just... I wanted to apologize for this morning." He lifted the brown paper bag in his right hand, its corded handle suspended from two fingers. And then he stopped talking and just stood there, waiting. It wasn't easy, but he was pretty sure it was the right approach. A guy like Caleb, prickly and proud, wasn't going to respond well to being pressured. Also, the larger of the two dogs was growling again, a low rumble that sounded like it was vibrating right out of the creature's chest into the ground beneath them. Confidence was nice, in theory, but damn, that was a big dog.

Finally, Caleb moved. "Settle down, Diesel," he said, and the dog flattened his ears as if suggesting that he'd prefer a different approach. "Diesel," Caleb said, still quietly but with more intensity, and the dog clearly heard the warning in his master's voice. Damn. It was kind of sexy, really. But there was no way Peter should be thinking like that. This was business.

So he put his best sincere smile on, the one that said *I'm friendly and professional*, not *I'd like to hear you talk to me in that tone while we're both naked.* He extended the bag toward Caleb, who took it cautiously.

He peered inside, then looked back up. "It's almost six o'clock at night. Did you really think I hadn't had breakfast yet?"

"No, I assumed you had. I thought you could have this tomorrow." Peter had done his best. He'd found the closest thing the town had to gourmet ground coffee and pastries, and if Caleb was used to better, Peter had no idea who the supplier was.

"I don't... I'm not really comfortable taking gifts from you." Caleb reached out toward Peter, the bag dangling from the end of his fingers.

Well, Peter hadn't actually expected it to be that easy. "I bought it with my own money, if that helps. It's a personal apology, not a corporate bribe." But the stubborn bastard kept his arm stretched out, and Peter finally leaned forward and took the bag back. He set it carelessly on the trunk of the car and held his hands out to the sides in an *I'm unarmed and want to make peace* gesture. "Coffee or not, I am truly sorry I made you uncomfortable. Frustrated, angry... whatever. I'm sorry. I realize that this is an emotional situation for everyone down here, especially for those who live closest to the site. I just... I really want to find a way to make this work for everyone."

"An 'emotional situation' that you want to make 'work for everyone'?" Caleb looked disgusted. Peter was getting a little tired of seeing that expression, but he swallowed his irritation.

"I know you don't believe that's possible, but I'm really pretty good at finding solutions to things. Working outside the box. And I was wrong this morning." He was pretty sure that statement would catch Caleb's interest, and, indeed, the man's delicate eyebrows arched inquiringly. Peter figured it was the best invitation he was going to get. "If you're not interested in hearing any more, I understand. But that's not the only reason I have for wanting to meet with you. I'm really hoping maybe you can give *me* some information. I'm hoping you can help me understand your objections and concerns, so I can do a better job of making sure we address them."

"You have trouble understanding people's concerns about noise, vibrations, water quality, and traffic? Really?"

"No, of course I understand the general principles. But, this morning—you said there was no way we could compensate you for any loss of enjoyment of your land. *That's* what I'm hoping to understand better." It was true, Peter realized. There was something about this man, his shyness contrasting with his passion, his deep brown eyes following Peter as if trying to figure *him* out; there was something intriguing there. "Obviously you're under no obligation, and I realize that you're busy. I realize that you don't like me. But I'd really appreciate any time you could spare. I really am trying to make this work."

Caleb was frowning now, and his fingers reached absently for the ears of the dog sitting at his feet. The smaller dog. The other one, the growling one... he hadn't given up on his intended prey. And, Peter was somewhat alarmed to notice, the creature had actually maneuvered himself around to get right between Peter and the open car door. He'd cut off the closest escape route, and it didn't seem accidental.

"It's not personal." Caleb's words didn't make sense at first, and Peter had to call his attention back from the dog he'd been trying not to stare at. Caleb frowned, as if thinking. "Not liking you. It's not personal. It's just—I don't like what you represent. What you're doing."

"I understand." And he did. He'd seen the same reaction so many times before. It might not make sense, but there were lots of people who were perfectly happy to shoot the messenger if they couldn't find a better target. At least Caleb was honest enough to admit it. "I think we can still work together, if you can just... I don't know." Time for another charming smile. "Can you pretend I'm someone else?"

"No." Judging by Caleb's expression, Peter figured he'd better ease off on the charm attempts. They obviously weren't working, and seemed to be making things worse. "But... yeah. Maybe I can try to make you understand." He looked at the dog who was still staring at Peter, and shook his head a little. "Ease off, Diesel. He's a guest."

The dog's ears twitched at his name, and Peter watched out of the corner of his eye as the animal cast a doubtful look in his owner's direction, then returned his gaze hopefully to Peter.

"No," Caleb said. "He's not a chew toy. Go find a stick. Go on." In a firmer voice, Caleb repeated, "Diesel, get a stick."

Another doubtful look, but the dog stood up and walked grumpily away. After a few steps, he broke into a slow trot that made his shoulder muscles roll like a weight lifter's.

"He's not aggressive," Caleb said. "I mean... he's just defending his territory."

"They're beautiful animals," Peter said, looking down at the dog at Caleb's feet. "Are you a bit friendlier, buddy?"

The dog looked up at his owner as if for permission, and Caleb nodded down at him. "It's okay, Diego. He's a—" He caught himself and looked up at Peter. "The word they know... the one I use... it doesn't mean anything, okay?"

Peter had no idea what was going on, but he nodded. "Okay...."

Caleb looked down at the animal. "Okay, Diego. He's a friend."

The change was almost instant. Peter could swear that the animal was smiling as he stood up and walked forward, his whole body wagging in a slow wave. The dog dropped his head as if bashful, but lifted it as Peter crouched down and reached a hand out in greeting. Peter wasn't prepared for the enthusiastic response. The dog rushed forward, trying to nuzzle in under Peter's chin or hug him or something, something that apparently required full-body contact and a hell of a lot of pressure. Peter lost his balance and rolled backward until his suit-wearing ass hit the dirty gravel of the driveway, and the dog celebrated the achievement with a series of enthusiastic full-tongue licks to Peter's face.

"Diego!" Caleb half yelled, rushing forward to haul the animal off.

"It's fine," Peter said, his face carefully tilted to avoid a French kiss from the dog. "He's great." The dog's fur was surprisingly soft under his fingers, and Peter found the magic spot on the animal's neck that made his heavy body relax with pleasure.

But Caleb was frantically pulling the animal away. "He's a menace. He doesn't understand how big he is."

"No, he's fine. No harm done." But Peter let himself rest on the ground a little longer, until Caleb had the dog dragged away and returned to offer Peter a hand up. It was a good strategy, Peter rationalized. A little guilt, and a little physical contact... it was the start of a useful relationship. A strategy. It had nothing to do with Peter's surprising interest in knowing what Caleb's skin felt like. And if Peter let himself lean forward a little, enough to get a quick whiff of the other man's scent, well—that was physics, or something, making it easier to stand up. That was all.

Caleb released Peter's hand as quickly as he possibly could, more quickly than seemed natural, and Peter hoped he hadn't pushed too far with whatever the hell he was doing. Or, even more, hoped he hadn't just outed himself in some way. In the city, sure, he was out. He kept his sex life away from his professional life, but he didn't hide anything. Down here in the back woods, though, Peter didn't want to be stupid about it. He was here to make peace, not to get himself beaten up. He looked around quickly for the mean dog, and the sight that met him was enough to distract him from his worries.

"Whoa! That's... you told him to get a *stick*, didn't you?" The dog was dragging a tree trunk across the lawn toward them. It must have been six feet long, probably nearly a foot in diameter, and the only reason the dog could move it at all was that it had a stub of a branch sticking out as a mouth-hold.

"Diesel's an overachiever," Caleb said. "It keeps him busy." He looked down at the other dog, and released his grip on the collar. "Diego, go help!" He waved his arm in the appropriate direction. "Go on, Diego, get Diesel!"

Diego gave one wistful look in Peter's direction, as if hoping for the chance to knock him over again, but then bounded happily in the direction Caleb had indicated. He arrived at the work site and immediately latched on to the same branch Diego was gripping and started tugging mightily... in the opposite direction.

"That should keep them busy for a while," Caleb said, turning back toward Peter. "I'm sorry, again. About him knocking you over."

"No problem."

Caleb squinted as if weighing his options. Apparently he decided in Peter's favor, and said, "You really want to know why this place is irreplaceable? Why you can't just 'compensate' me for its loss?"

"I really do."

Another assessing look, then Caleb nodded as if he'd committed to a course of action. "Fine." He started for the house.

Peter fell in behind him, hoping it was what he was supposed to do. He hadn't exactly been invited, but he hadn't been told to stay put, either. For someone who could speak so passionately, Caleb was surprisingly inept at the more casual forms of communication. Or maybe he just wasn't making much of an effort with Peter.

They approached the house, and Peter tried to see it as Caleb must. It was a fairly typical Ontario farmhouse, the sloped side of the roof facing forward with a steeply pitched gable in the middle, a porch stretching out along the entire front side. It looked like it was in good shape, but there was nothing remarkable about it. Peter followed his host up the stairs, careful to keep his eyes off the ass in front of him, and stopped on the porch to follow Caleb's gaze out across the lawn and struggling dogs to the forest, the trees covered in a soft green haze of tiny new leaves. Peter could tell he was expected to say something. "You've kept it really well maintained," he offered.

That didn't seem to be what Caleb had been looking for. He turned and opened the door, and Peter wiped his feet carefully on the mat before they stepped inside. Caleb flipped a light switch, and Peter looked around. The inside had been pretty extensively renovated, a lot of the walls removed to open things up, and some of the furniture was fantastic: solid, heavy wood pieces that felt rustic and sophisticated at the same time.

"You're a carpenter, right? A cabinetmaker? Is this your work?"

Caleb nodded. "But furniture can move."

"Well, yeah." Peter felt like he was being asked to make Caleb's argument for him. "But it really suits this place. Looks good here."

"That's not the important part," Caleb insisted. He stepped forward and rested his hand on one of the vertical beams. As Peter looked closer he saw that the wood was rough, as if it had been cut in chunks rather than sawed. Caleb nodded. "This is original to the house. My great-great-grandfather built the place... the front part, at least. He and his brothers cleared the land and kept the best trees for building, and my great-great-grandfather hand-hewed all the logs into square beams. The trees had been growing for... I don't know, a hundred years? Probably more. This was virgin forest, and they would have used the biggest trees for beams." He looked at Peter as if checking that he was following along, and Peter made sure his face reflected his interest. He had no idea what other expression was desired, but apparently the one he came up with was enough, and Caleb continued. "So, say, a hundred and fifty years old. Then my great-great-grandfather cut it down, used it to build this house, and it's stood here, giving shelter to generation after generation of my family, for another hundred and fifty years."

Caleb looked at Peter again and seemed to be encouraged by what he saw. He stepped forward into the living room and laid his hand on the rough stone hearth. "They probably had a fireplace when they first got here. Stoves are more efficient, but they're heavy and expensive, so it probably would have waited a few years. So my great-great-grandmother would have cooked all the meals here, heated water for washing, sewed by the light of the fire—a fire that was burning logs that grew on this land. They used the ashes to make soap, and threw what was left back into the forest, and it sank into the soil, grew into trees, and got cut down and burned again, maybe by my grandma and grandpa." He nodded to the neatly stacked pile of firewood on the hearth. "And maybe that's the same ashes, back round again."

His fingers found a line in one of the stones and traced over it almost reverently. "They got a stove at some point, maybe more than one, and when I was a kid there was a big monster of a thing in here. When it got going, we'd have all the windows open to cool the place down. My grandma wanted a prettier room, so my grandpa tore that stove out, and he built this fireplace by hand." Caleb's grin was quick and sweet. "I can still remember it. I was... I don't know, four or five? I really wanted to help, but of course I couldn't do anything useful. Stones are heavy. But he let me help mix the mortar. And there's... I don't know where, thank God... there's a couple of my brother's teeth in there, somewhere. Grandpa said it was even better than putting them under your pillow. And the Tooth Fairy came, and she left the money on the hearth." His look now was pointed. "This hearth isn't going anywhere. That chimney... every stone carefully placed by a man who was already exhausted from working in town *and* trying to keep the farm running, but who wanted to make his wife happy... that chimney is part of this house, and part of this land, and part of my family. There is no fucking way you can compensate me for losing it. Do you understand that?"

Peter nodded slowly. "I do." And he did. He'd been raised in a series of apartments, and had nothing in his own experience that compared with Caleb's ancestral home, but that didn't mean he couldn't see how a place like this would resonate with someone lucky enough to have it. "But there's no reason to believe the quarry will make this property unlivable," he said. For the first time he could remember, he felt a little guilty about trying to do his job. He wasn't lying, exactly, but he was coming closer to it than he wanted. "I know it sounds bad, having an industry next door instead of a farm. But, really... we bought almost two thousand acres from the Deans. They were running a large-scale, *industrial* farming operation, with all the chemicals that entails. Fertilizers, herbicides, pesticides... don't try to tell me they were operating that place on anything close to an organic basis, because I've seen the numbers."

Peter wished he couldn't see Caleb's expression. The cautious optimism that had started to show when Peter had said he understood was completely gone, replaced with an almost desperate defiance. "They weren't organic, no. But they were a *farm*." He looked out the window at the falling dusk, then back at Peter. "Do you still want to understand?" There was a challenge in his voice.

"Yes, of course." There was no other answer.

"You're going to get muddy."

That wasn't great news; Peter had yet to find a dry cleaner in the town, and he was running out of fresh business clothes. But he'd come this far. "Okay," he said, trying to sound unconcerned.

"Come on, then," Caleb said, and he headed further into the house, through a large, open kitchen, into a mudroom, and then out the back door. They hadn't gone far before the dogs bounded over to meet them, and Peter quickly hid his triumphant grin when he saw the paper bag in Diesel's mouth. The *empty* paper bag that had formerly held Peter's rejected peace offering.

Caleb took a little longer to understand what the dog was carrying. He took the soggy paper from Diesel's mouth, looked at it, then looked at Peter with a look of almost comical horror.

Peter grinned and raised his hands quickly. "If you didn't want the pastries, I was just going to throw them out anyway, I expect. No harm done. I hope they didn't eat the coffee, though. I have no idea what effect caffeine has on dogs."

Caleb squinted toward the driveway. "They probably chewed up the wrapper and spread the coffee all over the place." He turned back to Peter. "I'm really sorry."

And again, Peter felt an uncharacteristic flash of guilt. He'd deliberately put the bag in harm's way, right on the edge of the trunk where it could easily fall off or be reached by a curious snout. He'd wanted Caleb to feel a bit guilty, a bit indebted, and he'd gotten what he wanted. So why the hell was he feeling guilty himself? "Seriously, don't worry about it." He gestured in the direction they'd been traveling. "What did you want to show me?"

Caleb gave him one more doubtful look, but then started moving again. He was walking quickly, and Peter almost had to jog to keep up. "Chickens, and a goat. And the beef cattle," Caleb said, nodding toward the ramshackle barn. "A couple scrub quarter horses, just for messing around on. They all live on pasture, mostly, with a bit of grain and hay in the winter." He didn't seem inclined to stop and show off his livestock, but they slowed down when they reached the tree line. "Apples," Caleb said, and Peter realized that they were in an orchard. "Pears." Caleb gestured. "And peaches. Those are nuts, over there. My grandmother planted most of them, but I've added a few more."

Peter was about to say that the quarry shouldn't affect the trees at all, but Caleb was still moving, and Peter realized that the orchard wasn't their real destination. They continued, the dogs bounding ahead, through the fruit trees and into the forest, following a path that was wide enough for them to walk side by side, although they didn't. Caleb had been right about the mud, and Peter could feel his shoes getting heavier as they collected samples of the land's precious soil.

After a few minutes of walking they stopped and Caleb stepped aside, as if inviting Peter to move up beside him. They were on the top of a rough, rocky hill, looking out at smooth farmland that seemed to stretch forever. The dogs were halfway across the field, intent on stalking something.

Caleb's voice was soft. "There used to be a lake here. You know... prehistorically. Just after the glaciers dumped all that gravel you guys are after. But the lake covered it all, and over the years, the sediment built up as the lake turned into a swamp, and then dry land. Flat, fertile land." He kicked a rock at his foot. "This property, it would have been an island. Scraped down to bedrock by the glaciers, but it held on. It didn't get washed away." Peter had the idea that maybe Caleb was identifying with that aspect of his land, but it didn't seem like the time to push. Caleb's voice was stronger when he continued, waving an arm out at the land in front of them. "The rest of it... it's been giving people food for a hundred and fifty years. Longer than that, really, 'cause there was a good-sized native population in the area before the Europeans arrived."

Caleb moved, then, shuffling down the rough slope with the confident ease of someone who'd followed the same path a thousand times before. Peter did his best to follow. By the time he reached the bottom, Caleb had walked to the edge of the field and was crouched down, his fingers gently touching something on the ground.

He looked up as Peter reached him. "Winter wheat," he explained. "They plant it in the fall, and it sprouts and grows and hangs on under the snow, then grows fast and hard with all the moisture in the spring. Gets harvested just after the first cut of hay, usually." He was looking down at the small green plants as if they were miracles, and Peter realized that to Caleb, they were.

"What do they use it for?" Peter didn't really care, but he needed to say something.

"Flour, mostly. If something goes wrong and it's not a good harvest, it might just be animal feed. But those animals get turned into meat, so one way or the other, they use it to *feed people*." Caleb straightened up. "You're right about the chemicals. But you're wrong if you think that means this farm isn't still a part of nature. A hell of a lot closer to it than your damn hole in the ground. This soil has been feeding people for generations, part of the same cycle that I was talking about with the ashes and the trees for my firewood. It's great soil. Great farmland. And you're going to scrape it all off and dump it somewhere, because you want to get at the stupid little rocks down beneath it."

"The stupid little rocks are needed for roads. And buildings. It'd be nice if we could all live in our ancestral manors, but most of us don't have that luxury. There are millions of people in this province, and they don't just need homes—they need schools and hospitals and a shitload of other things that are all built with concrete. And concrete needs gravel." Peter shook his head. He didn't usually get this worked up, and it wasn't good for business. He looked at the green shoots in the field, and crouched down to lift a few gently with his fingers, as he had seen Caleb do. "People need food too. I get that. But... what's the point of having the wheat if you don't have roads to get it to the market, or even the mill?"

"Why does it have to be *this* gravel?"

"Where are we going to go that people aren't going to have

the same arguments you have here? Maybe way up north, but what's the environmental cost of shipping something as heavy as gravel all that distance?"

They looked at each other for a long time. There was nothing left to say. Finally, Caleb turned and started toward the hill. It was almost full dark now, and Peter struggled to keep up. The hill seemed more slippery on the way up, as if the darkness had somehow made the mud more liquid. Peter felt a strange sense of inevitability rather than alarm when his feet slipped out from under him. He fell heavily on his hands and knees but couldn't find his balance, and then he was slipping down the hill, flat on his belly, his hands scrabbling uselessly at the muddy path.

It wasn't dangerous. Not really. But Peter still felt a sense of relief when his fingers closed on the warm skin of Caleb's hand, stretched out to catch him and stop his fall.

"Shit," Caleb said.

"I'm hoping it's just mud," Peter replied. He tried for another of his charming grins, and this time, for the first time, Caleb reluctantly smiled back.

CHAPTER SEVEN

THE whole thing would have been much easier if the bastard hadn't been quite so nice. Or quite so gorgeous. One or the other and Caleb figured he could have resisted. He glanced behind him. Peter was struggling along gamely, walking a little stiff-legged as if trying to keep the wet, muddy fabric of his clothes away from his more tender skin. If Peter'd been a friend, Caleb would have laughed at him, but he was a stranger, practically an enemy, and apparently that meant Caleb had to feel bad about it all.

"Not much further," he said in what he hoped was an encouraging way.

"And then I get to sit in my car and let it all congeal while I drive back to the motel." Peter didn't sound like he was complaining. It was more like he was inviting Caleb to laugh at him. With him.

"You can clean up at my place, if you want. Shower, or whatever. You're taller than I am, obviously, but I could loan you some sweat pants or something. And I wear my shirts pretty loose, so you could probably fit into one of them." They were close to the house now, close enough that when Caleb turned around, he could see Peter's face clearly in the lights from the back porch. Peter looked like a man who had just been invited to get naked in Caleb's house, and who wasn't totally against the idea.

But that was ridiculous. Caleb jerked his head back around

so the flush on his face couldn't be seen. Projection, that's what a pop psychologist would call it. *Wishful thinking* is what his mom would have said. *In your dreams, Caleb.* He could almost hear her laughter, made rough by too many years of smoking and hating.

"No, I don't want to impose."

Caleb didn't turn around, and refused to let himself analyze the strange tone in Peter's voice. "It wouldn't be an imposition. I got you dirty; I can help you get clean."

"You've already helped." Caleb had stopped walking at the bottom of the porch steps; he knew Peter was right behind him, waiting for him to turn around. He complied, and was rewarded with another smile. "You've helped me to understand. I'm not really sure what I can do about it, not yet, but…. You may not share my love of information, but to me, it's important."

"I didn't give you any *information*," Caleb corrected. "Geology? What crops your land grows? You knew all that already."

Peter's nod was slow and thoughtful. "Yeah, I guess I did. But I didn't get it, you know? I guess you're right; I had the information. But I didn't have the understanding. The perspective. That's what you helped me with."

Jesus, he was a beautiful man. Just physically, Caleb hastened to remind himself, and then felt guilty; Peter had been pretty damn sweet about the eaten pastries, and the mud, and Caleb's crazy quasi-mystical babbling about the importance of the house and the land. So maybe he was a good guy, but that didn't mean he was Caleb's friend. The man was in town to do a job. He was in town to try to make Caleb and everyone else feel good about their lives being torn apart.

"Okay, then, we're even," Caleb said. He needed to get the hell out of there. "Diesel! Diego! Let's go—dinner!" He edged past Peter and climbed the stairs to the porch. There was no way he was going to repeat his offer of a place to clean up. He had satisfied the requirements of courtesy, and that was all Caleb was ready for. "Thanks for coming out." That wasn't quite what he wanted to say. "For listening. I don't... I think we both know it's not going to make a damn bit of difference. But it was nice of you to go through the motions." The dogs appeared out of the darkness and bounded past Peter as if he were a part of the landscape, their attention on their promised dinner. It was a welcome distraction, and Caleb opened the door for them before looking back at Peter. "You can go around the side of the house, there, to get to the driveway. It's pretty well lit."

"Thank you." Peter looked like maybe he had something more to say, but he thought better of it and turned to go. "I hope I'll see you around." And there it was again, that little bit of... something.

"Yeah, maybe," Caleb managed to respond, then he stepped inside and closed the door behind him. It wasn't like it was out of the question for Peter to be gay; lots of people were, after all. No, the part that was ridiculous was Caleb thinking someone like Peter might be interested in someone like him, even just for a quick trick. Caleb might be the only show in town, at least in terms of out gay men, but they weren't *that* far from the city. Peter could do a hell of a lot better with just a little driving. The whole thing was ridiculous.

Caleb scooped a few yogurt containers of kibble into the dogs' bowls and left them eating in the mudroom; Diesel wolfing his dinner like he'd never been fed, Diego nibbling daintily. Caleb knew from experience that Diesel wouldn't steal his brother's food, and also knew that Diego would leave a few pieces of kibble in his bowl for Diesel to enjoy at the end. It had never been clear whether the remnants were meant as a bribe or a gift, but Caleb liked to think it was the latter. He certainly didn't like to think that Diego wanted to save the food for later, and hadn't learned, after all this time, that he would always lose his snack to his brother.

It was time to worry about his own dinner, Caleb decided, and he pulled off his muddy boots and headed for the kitchen. He was thinking about the mud all down Peter's tailored suit, the way the wetness had made the man's shirt cling to his lean torso, and he was startled when he heard a voice from over by the kitchen table.

"You out saying goodbye to the Dean place?" It was Trevor, sitting at Caleb's table, drinking Caleb's beer, and smirking at Caleb's surprise. "Was that the gravel guy you were talking to? What the hell happened to him?"

"He fell down," Caleb said. "Slipped. What are you doing here?"

"Just thought I'd drop in and say 'hi.' See what you were up to."

"You need money?" Caleb hated himself for being so cynical, but in the past he'd ended up hating himself for trusting his brother too much; this way would at least be easier on his self-respect, if not his bank account.

"Sure, if you've got some lying around." Trevor smiled as if he was joking, but Caleb kept his own expression neutral, and Trevor finally sighed. "I thought we should talk about the place. About selling it. You know you aren't going to want to stay here, not with that mess going in next door, and... well, yeah, I could use the money."

Caleb didn't say anything at first. Instead he went to the fridge, found a beer of his own, opened it, and took a long pull of amber coolness. He inhaled deeply, thought about what he wanted to say, and took another swallow. Then he turned and walked over to the kitchen table. The chairs were wood, made in Caleb's own shop, and most of the time he took satisfaction in their sturdiness. But tonight, he just sank into the seat and stared at his brother. "You don't own the property. You know that."

"I don't know that at all! What are you talking about?" Trevor's expression was familiar; that same golden, smiling, daring mask that he wore whenever he was trying to charm somebody, or fool them. Diego trotted in then, tail waving happily at the sight of a visitor, and Trevor obligingly rubbed the dog's ears. Diesel, a few steps behind, sat down a couple of steps away, watchful, as usual.

The distraction gave Caleb a few moments to control his irritation and make his voice as light as possible. "Come on, Trevor. We made a deal."

"This is my *home*, Caleb. Mom left it to both of us!"

Caleb wondered whether Trevor was on something. It had been meth, the last time he'd been busted. He seemed too calm for that now, but there was a weird energy around him that Caleb almost hoped wasn't natural. "She left it to us, and then I bought you out. Jesus, Trevor, do you really think I'm going to forget about that? I'm still making mortgage payments every month, paying off the money I borrowed to give to you."

"You took advantage." Trevor didn't sound like he was accusing; it was more like he was gently scolding a misbehaving youngster. "That contract... it can be cancelled. Breached. Whatever. Erased, because I wasn't in sound mind and body when I signed it." Trevor swallowed the last of his beer and leaned back in his chair with a satisfied air. "I was battling addiction, and I have the medical records to prove it."

"You're battling *reality*, Trevor. You had a lawyer; this was totally above board. And what the hell are you thinking? Let's say the contract *was* invalid, which it wasn't. But say it was. You'd have to give me back the money I gave you, and there's no way you have that kind of cash lying around. You think you're going to get half the house *and* the money I gave you to buy that half of the house? You're crazy."

"It wasn't a fair deal. The house is worth way more than you paid me for it." He stood up, and his movements were smooth and graceful, not jerky and random like they'd been when he was on meth. Caleb watched as his brother crossed the kitchen floor and opened the fridge to find another beer. Trevor turned and smiled, and his face was calm and easy, just as it had been when they were children together. "You know what's fair, Caleb. We're family, and this is a family house. When you sell to the gravel people, you need to give me my share."

"You're getting ahead of things, here. I'm not going to sell. I'm going to hang on and see if I can make it work." This was what Caleb needed to be talking about. Trevor was right; he was the only family Caleb had left, and *if* Caleb sold the house, he would probably give Trevor whatever portion of his half Caleb hadn't already paid. But that was all theoretical, because Caleb had no intention of abandoning his home.

Apparently, Trevor wasn't accepting that plan. "It's going to be a war zone, Caleb. You're a happy hermit out here, with your carpentry and your animals. But it's not going to be like that anymore. You should sell now, when we can get a good price, and spare yourself the trouble of watching it all go to hell."

"I appreciate your concern for my well-being. Really." Caleb didn't think he let too much bitterness into his voice. "And if you need money that bad, I can probably find some." He knew it was pointless, but he tried anyway. "Or if you're looking for work, I could hook you up, at least part-time."

"I'm not taking a job sweeping up after my baby brother," Trevor said firmly, and took another swig of the alcohol purchased by his baby brother's hard work.

"Are you working anywhere else? Anything on the horizon?"

"You know, it'd be nice if we could have, like, a family visit, instead of an interrogation." Trevor looked hopefully toward the fridge. "Have you had dinner yet?"

And that was that. Trevor was ready to move on, and Caleb couldn't really think of a reason to resist. So he stood up and headed for the fridge, Trevor helpfully returning to the table and taking his seat again as he watched Caleb cook. They talked about mutual acquaintances and Trevor spun glorious tales of his own exploits and Caleb listened and laughed at the appropriate places. Trevor was his big brother. Trevor had, more or less, stood by Caleb when he'd come out. And Trevor had been more damaged by their childhood than Caleb had. For both of them, their grandparents' farm had been the only source of stability in a world of swirling confusion; for Caleb, the farm had been enough, but Trevor had always needed more. So now, if Trevor wanted a dinner, a few beers, and an uncritical audience, Caleb was happy to provide. But he'd be damned if he'd give up his home without a fight, no matter which side of the battle Trevor was on.

CHAPTER EIGHT

"HE WANTS things to stay the same. That's totally understandable, right?" Peter was bouncing ideas around, and Riva was, as usual, paying only cursory attention to him. She picked critically at her granola while Peter paced around the motel room they were using as an office. It had doors connecting to both of their rooms, so they'd formed a sort of suite with the office in the middle. It wasn't ritzy, but it was functional. It would have been easier to set up an office in the old Dean home, but Peter didn't think it would give the right impression to the community. People didn't need to have the changed circumstances shoved down their throats. "He's lived there his whole life. He's really in touch with the land... all that stuff. So, yeah, he doesn't want things to change."

But Riva was frowning at him, now, instead of her cereal. "Not his whole life, I don't think. I was talking to people yesterday." She cupped her hand under her dark bob, indicating that she'd followed her standard practice of getting her hair done and encouraging gossip during the process. "They said his mom moved them around a lot when they were kids. Her parents owned the house, but they kicked her out, reconciled, kicked her out again... that sort of thing. Apparently she was a pretty heavy drinker, rarely employed." Her frown turned to an inquisitive look. "And did you know he's gay? Apparently he came out right after high school. Everyone expected him to move up to the city, but he stuck around, started his business here. They say it's because he had to look after his mom, and then his brother."

That was a lot of new information. Peter tried to focus on the part of it that was relevant to his business interests, and ignore his stupid burst of inappropriate excitement. "So the home was probably his main source of stability, making it even more important to him. The grandparents and mother are...?"

"Deceased. The mother was a late-in-life baby, so the grandparents were a good age. The mother went pretty early. 'Cancer of the everything' is how it was described to me."

"And now it's just him and the brother? No father?"

"Nobody mentioned one." Riva set her bowl on the table. "We talked about the Diefenbakers a bit too. Apparently they have two sons and a daughter, but none of the kids is too interested in farming, at least not right now. So they'd be easy to buy out, if it came to that."

If it came to that. If the quarry made the neighbors' lives so miserable that they were forced to abandon their homes. "What are the chances of it being that bad? You're the engineer. You know the plans."

Riva raised an eyebrow at him. "You know better than that. Since when is it about facts, or anything absolute? There's going to be changes. If people go into it looking to be disturbed, they're going to be disturbed."

"And what if he's not looking to be disturbed, just trying to live his life?"

"'He'? Mr. Diefenbaker?" Riva looked confused for a moment before her frown faded into a grin. "Oh. Caleb Sinclair. He's pretty cute, Peter."

"That's not what this is about," Peter protested. "It's business. You said we could buy out the Diefenbakers. We've already got good property buffers on two sides of the property, and the highway's on the third side, so the people there are more used to noise. Caleb Sinclair is the one most likely to be upset about this."

"*And* he's pretty cute," Riva said. "And he works with his hands—creates things. That's sexy, and you know it."

Peter tried to ignore her attempts to derail his train of thought. "How much community support is he likely to get, if he fights? I mean, there was a lot of hostility the other night, at the meeting, but there wasn't a focus, yet. Carol Diefenbaker was the closest, but there really wasn't anyone stepping up and leading. Is he likely to do that?"

"I got the idea he's a bit... controversial, in the community. The gay thing, mostly. And apparently right after he came out, he got beat up pretty bad. Gay bashed. He identified the guys, pressed charges, and some promising young citizens ended up with criminal records. You figure that there were four or five of them, and each of them has family in the area... that's a good number of people carrying a grudge." She waited to see how Peter was taking her analysis, then continued. "But it sounds like a lot of people like him too. He teaches an evening course in woodworking, and two of the women at the salon had taken it. Made salad bowls, apparently. They said he was lovely."

Lovely. It was such an old-fashioned word, but, damn it, it kind of fit. After all, with his connection to the land and his woodworking, Caleb was kind of an old-fashioned guy. But Peter needed to keep his mind on business. "He's unreachable. There's no way we're going to win him over. I want to go after Carol Diefenbaker. If we get her on board we've got a strong ally, *and* we've eliminated a strong opponent."

"So... how do you want to do that?"

"I think you should talk to her. We made the standard contributions to all the community organizations when we first bought the land, but now we need to ratchet it up. She's involved in 4H and the town library... find out if she's got any pet projects either place. Talk to her, but keep it casual. Just two gals having tea, or whatever."

"Yeah, having tea. That's what we gals do, while you men are out shooting buffalo."

"I've always wondered. Thanks for clearing that up."

"No problem." She paused long enough to make it clear that she was about to change the subject, then said, "You don't ever want to just... ram it through? Just tell them, 'the Aggregate Act is grossly in favor of resource extraction and we can essentially do anything we want to because of it, so sit down and shut up and stop making us spend time and money on trying to win you all over'? You never want to do that?"

"These are their homes, Riva. They have every right to be upset. I don't want them to sit down and shut up."

"Yeah, I know, Saint Peter. I get that. But, what I'm saying is... these are their homes. Don't they have the *right* to be angry? Don't they have the *right* to hate us for sweeping in here and changing everything? It just seems... it's bad enough that we're going to do it. But now we have to brainwash them into being *happy* about it? Isn't that kind of adding insult to injury? Isn't it disrespectful?"

Peter remembered Caleb's face when he'd mocked Peter's words about finding a solution that would work for everyone. The man was definitely resisting Peter's attempted brainwashing, and Peter couldn't blame him. Still, "It's what we do, Riva. The company wants good community relations. We make that happen."

"Yeah," she said, and she was back to being resigned, almost sad. She didn't say the words, but Peter could hear them as clearly as if she had. *Is this all there is?*

He frowned at her, not sure whether to be impatient or concerned. "The gravel needs to come from somewhere. And like you said, if people go into it with a bad attitude they're going to be unhappy. But if they go in with a good attitude, they'll be fine. We're just helping them go in with a good attitude." Riva was still looking at him, but he turned away and busied himself with some papers. He believed what he'd just said. It had been his guiding principle through years of doing his job all over the continent. It was true, and right. But somehow it was starting to feel empty. It was still true, but it was by no means all there was.

He snorted impatiently and shoved the papers away. "Damn it, Riva, do you have to do this right *now*? Can we not just get through this job, and then... I don't know, you can take a vacation, and do your soul-searching in the tropics or something." He didn't have to look at her to know what her expression would be, and he felt like an insensitive ass. He sighed and added, "And then you can come back and tell me what you've found." Now he could glance over and give her a regretful smile. "It's not that I don't care. I'm interested, and I'm starting to understand. I just... I need to get through this job."

"Or maybe you don't," she suggested, her voice soft. "Maybe neither one of us does."

"Don't drag me into your crisis of faith, sweetheart. I'm fine. I got a little distracted for a second, but I'm still on the job. And so are you." Peter knew that Riva was familiar with his techniques, but he gave her the charming smile anyhow. "You can finish this project with me, right? I mean, once we're done here, you can do what you need to do, and you absolutely have my support. But can you stick with me until then?"

"Peter...." Riva set her bowl on the counter of the kitchenette and crossed the room to stand next to him. Her hand was warm on his shoulder. "Yeah. I can stick it out. And I'm not trying to drag you into anything, honestly. I just thought you might want to come with me on your own."

"I'm fine," he said, and he gave her another full-powered smile. "I'm good where I am." He didn't know whether she believed him or not, but she didn't argue, so he called it a victory. "So, you can talk to Mrs. Diefenbaker? You know the drill."

Before Riva could answer, there was a knock at the door.

Peter raised an eyebrow at her, asking if she was expecting anyone, and she shrugged a negative response. Peter went to the door and opened it to find Trevor Sinclair standing there. The resemblance to the brother was fading as Peter got to know both of them better. Their personalities were so different that the physical was being overshadowed.

"Trevor. Good morning." Peter didn't invite the other man in, but he stepped aside as Trevor moved forward.

"I talked to Caleb, like I said I would." Trevor smiled widely, and Peter wondered if he needed to spend a bit more time practicing his own smile in the mirror. It looked pretty awful when charming was attempted and not achieved. But Trevor seemed oblivious to Peter's hesitation. "We're interested in hearing an offer." Another smile. "Honestly, I thought it would be harder to convince Caleb. He seems to really like you, man!" And now the eyebrows were waggling. The man's face was almost manically mobile.

"I didn't really get that impression," Peter said dryly. "He seemed to want me off the property as soon as possible."

"He said you were all muddy. He said he felt terrible about it, and that he was starting to realize you're really a good guy. He said he trusts you." Now Trevor leaned in as if telling a secret. "To be honest, I think… well, he asked me to handle all the negotiations. He said he'd sign, you know, if the price is right, but he said he didn't want to see you or hear from you." Trevor held up his hands as if warding off an imaginary blow. "I know, that sounds as if he doesn't like you! But I know my brother, and… I think maybe he likes you a little *too* much, if you know what I mean." He frowned. "That doesn't freak you out, does it? Did you know he's a fag? Gay. Whatever. He's not going to start grabbing your ass or anything—he's pretty well-behaved, really. Doesn't talk about it all the time, or act all swishy. But, yeah, he gets crushes sometimes, and I help him out." Trevor seemed to expect Peter to admire him for his benevolence. "Like now. He's not comfortable seeing you, so he's asked me to handle it all. I can do that."

"Uh... okay." Peter couldn't do what he wanted to do. He was there representing the company, and the company did not want its representatives manhandling locals. Not even if the local was an annoying homophobe who really seemed to be trying to cheat his brother out of his share of the family home. Peter wished he'd cleared up the ownership the day before so he'd be able to shut this nonsense down with a little more authority. As ridiculous as the 'crush' nonsense was, Peter supposed there was a possibility, at least, that Caleb had asked his brother to act on his behalf. Then he remembered the way Caleb's hand had rested on the fireplace chimney as if trying to draw strength from it, the tenderness with which he'd touched the fragile shoots of winter wheat, and Peter knew without a doubt that Trevor was lying. "We'll need to deal with the registered owner of the property. If you can get yourself registered, that's fine. But until then... well, I'm not swishy, either, and I absolutely try not to grab strange men's asses, but for your brother I would seriously consider making an exception. So maybe it's best that *I* step back a little, so my crush doesn't get the better of *me*." He turned his head toward Riva, and saw her doing an excellent job of controlling her smirk. "Maybe you could take care of that for me, Riva? Give Mr. Sinclair a call and see what we can do to make this all work?"

"Absolutely," Riva said. Her smile was bright and innocent. "I'm happy to help you out with that, Peter. I know how hard it can be to behave rationally when all you can think about is a man's beautiful face, or his body...."

"The way he'd feel, pressed up against you...." Peter knew he was crossing a line, but he didn't seem to care, and Riva wasn't going to rat him out.

She was having far too much fun with it. "His hands: so strong, so tender, touching you in all the right places...."

And that was probably enough of the game, because damn it,

Caleb Sinclair *did* have strong hands, and there were quite a few places Peter would absolutely like to be touched. He needed to get a grip. No, not *a grip*. Something else. He needed to calm down and get back to business, that's what he needed to do. He shook his head as if clearing his thoughts, and the gesture was only partially theatrics for Trevor's benefit. "Okay, yeah. So, I can't be trusted, and Riva will handle things. She'll get in touch with your brother, since he's the registered owner, and then everything's clear. Everyone involved can be trusted." He tried not to emphasize the last words, but he was pretty sure Trevor caught the meaning anyway.

"I'm not going to be shut out of this decision—" Trevor started to say, and Peter could hear the beginnings of a righteous rant.

"Neither is your brother," he said softly. "If you have an ownership claim, or if you're his authorized agent, get something signed by him or by the courts, and we'll talk. Until then... I appreciate your interest in our project, and would be happy to provide you with any information you need. We're here to make sure the whole community is happy with our company and with its work in your region." Peter didn't even try to make his smile genuine, and he could tell Trevor noticed the difference.

"So that's how it's going to be?" Trevor wasn't bothering with attempted pleasantness anymore, either, and the difference was almost chilling. Peter found himself stepping sideways a little, and realized that he was getting between Trevor and Riva, making sure the other man's attention was only on him. "You don't want to be friendly?" Trevor snarled.

"I have no problem being friendly," Peter replied. "As I said, we're here to make sure everyone is happy. But when it comes to making deals, we need to be careful about the law. And the law is pretty clear, right now, that your brother is the only registered owner of the property. Sorry."

Trevor looked like he was searching for a comeback, but apparently the only one he could come up with was, "Fucking faggot." His voice was low and intense, and Peter could feel the wave of anger sweeping toward him.

He met it head-on. "That's right. So I guess you should probably be careful about being seen in a motel room with me, right?" He reached a long arm out around Trevor to open the outside door. The movement exposed Peter's torso to the man, and made him feel intensely vulnerable, but he'd be damned if he'd shift his body away from its spot between Trevor and Riva, and the door needed to be opened, so he took the chance.

And apparently he could read homophobic bullies pretty well, because he wasn't surprised when Trevor made his move: a quick step forward, a raised fist that wasn't actually swung, and a fierce look on his face. Peter heard Riva gasp, but was able to keep himself from reacting. No flinching. He remembered the high school rules clearly enough, although he wasn't impressed to be following them fifteen years after he'd graduated.

"Thanks for coming by," he said, his voice as calm and level as he could make it. "We're always happy to meet with members of the Rocky Creek community. But maybe next time you could call ahead and make an appointment. We want to be sure we have lots of time to spend with you."

Trevor didn't say anything in reply, but he stepped backward, out of the room, and Peter didn't feel even a little bad for shutting the door in the man's face.

"Fucking faggot," he heard through the doorway, and he managed to smile at Riva.

"Charming member of society," he said.

"A prince," she agreed. "The brother must be a damned saint to put up with him."

"No reason to believe the brother *does*."

"Except that this clown knew you'd been out there yesterday.

Knew you'd fallen in the mud. That's not the sort of thing that would come up in hostile conversation, right?"

That was an annoying observation. "Yeah. Damn." Peter realized that, while it would certainly be awkward if Caleb decided to be angry with the company for being rude to his brother, that wasn't really what was upsetting about the situation. Peter thought about Caleb, trying to deal with a brother who thought "fucking faggot" was some sort of intellectual argument, and wondered how the man managed. Riva had said that it seemed Caleb had stuck around, instead of running off to be gay and fabulous in the big city, because he was looking after his mother, and then his brother. Peter had seen Caleb at his home, and he was pretty sure the townspeople were wrong about the primary reason Caleb was still there. But even if looking after his brother was way down his list of priorities, it was still a sign of something pretty profound that it was on the list at all.

"Riva?" Peter said softly. It was stupid, and he knew it, but for some reason he didn't seem to care. "I changed my mind. I'll take care of Caleb Sinclair, okay?"

He expected something sharper than her sweet, accepting smile. "Yeah. Okay." She looked as if she knew she shouldn't push it but just couldn't help herself, and she said, "This *isn't* all there is, Peter."

He was tempted to respond with some dramatic roar of frustration, but her face was too sweetly hopeful for him to startle her. Also, he was beginning to think she was right. Maybe.

"Okay," he said noncommittally, "if you say so."

"I absolutely do," she said, and she crossed the floor in a few steps and then stood on tiptoe to plant a quick kiss on his cheek. "And you do too."

She looked at him seriously, as if reading his thoughts, then nodded. "Yeah. You do. You just don't know it yet."

CHAPTER NINE

CALEB had ignored the message from The Gravel Guy. That's what he wanted to call him. The Gravel Guy. Not Peter Carr, and certainly not just Peter. He wasn't a human being, wasn't an incredibly gorgeous man, he was just... The Gravel Guy. And Caleb had ignored his message. Whatever The Gravel Guy wanted, Caleb wasn't interested. He had his own concerns.

So he tried to ignore the jolt of excitement that he felt as he pulled into his long driveway and saw the sedan waiting for him. And he tried even harder to ignore the rush of cold disappointment when he realized that the car didn't belong to The Gravel Guy after all. It was the second day in a row he'd come home to find a Dean sitting on his porch, but the second seemed likely to be the more challenging.

"Hi, Sarah," he said as he headed up the stairs. Matt's wife wasn't as familiar with the place as Matt was, and hadn't let the dogs outside. Caleb could hear Diesel's outraged growling through the door, partnered with Diego's excited whines. "Give me a second, okay?"

"Yeah, of course. Sorry for getting them worked up."

"If it wasn't you, it would have been a squirrel, or a gust of wind or something. They really don't like being shut up all day." Caleb opened the front door and greeted the dogs, then stepped aside as they rushed over to say hello to Sarah. They knew her, and Caleb wasn't worried about aggression, but he realized too late that she might be feeling a little fragile, and not ready for greetings from two rambunctious hounds. But she smiled as she leaned over to pet them, and they wriggled as happily as they had when they were little puppies meeting her for the first time. Caleb wished Peter could see Diesel like this, and realize that he wasn't a threat. And then Caleb wished he hadn't forgotten his resolution. Who the hell cared what The Gravel Guy thought about Caleb's dog?

"They've missed you," he said.

"Of course they have. Puppies need a female influence. Right, boys?" The dogs smiled at her in agreement. She spoiled them a little longer, then patted their ribcages decisively. "All right, critters. Enough for now. Go get a stick!"

The dogs looked at Caleb for confirmation, and he nodded. "Yeah! Get a stick! Go get it!"

The dogs bounded off toward the forest, and Caleb returned his attention to his visitor. "I guess I shouldn't offer you a beer.... Do you want... I don't know. Honestly, I've only got beer, coffee, or water. Sorry."

"No, I'm fine. Don't worry about it." Sarah's smile seemed sincere, and Caleb started to relax. He and Sarah had never really spent much time together without Matt being around, but they got along just fine. She was a friend.

"I hope you don't mind me coming out. I just... Matt told me that he told you. About... you know. About us trying again. And I just really wanted to...." She stopped and took a deep breath, and Caleb realized that she was working to keep from crying. Her trouble pulled him out of himself, and he realized it was just as strange for her to be out here visiting her husband's best friend as it was for him to be receiving her.

He settled into the chair next to hers, and they both stared at the forest as he reached out and found her hand where it sat on the armrest. "He told me," he confirmed. "I'm sending good thoughts your way."

Sarah's abdomen was still completely flat, but she laid her free hand against it, fingers spread out protectively. Caleb had a flash of what she would look like in the future, her belly stretched and round, her hand in just the same position as she felt the baby kicking. It was so vivid it felt more like a premonition than a simple act of imagination, but he didn't share it with her. After all the other times, he didn't want to do anything to give her false hope.

"I'm worried about him," Sarah said quietly. "He's so tense about the baby, and then all this stuff with the stupid gravel pit... it's too much. People he's known all his life walking past him without saying hello. What has he done to deserve that?"

"He talked to you about it?"

"He thought I didn't know!" She almost laughed, but settled on a tender smile. "He thinks I'm so naïve."

"I think he thought you were... preoccupied."

"But not totally blind." She sat up a little straighter. "And that's why I'm here. Because I see what's going on, and I don't like it, and I'm going to do something about it. But I'm not quite sure what, yet, so I wanted to talk some ideas over with you."

"Um... okay. But are you sure you want to get involved? Shouldn't you be... I don't know, resting? Gestating?"

"The gestation doesn't take a lot of mental effort, Caleb. And I want to be busy. Not frantic, but, you know... I don't want to think about the baby all the time. I can't. I need to just relax and let things happen."

That made sense, maybe. He wasn't really in a position to judge, but at least he could support. "Yeah, okay. So, what are you thinking about?"

"Well, here's the thing. My main goal... selfishly, you understand, so the emphasis is on *my*... is to get people off Matt's back. They're not being as mean to me, and it doesn't really bother me anyway. So that's what I want to do. And to do that, I could just make it clear that Matt's a good guy, that his parents didn't know what they were selling the land *for*, and whatever else would make people realize they're being stupid." She looked for Caleb's nod of support, got it, and continued. "But it occurred to me that Matt and I have a very dear friend who is going to be seriously affected by the quarry, and who might be interested in actually fighting it. And it occurred to me that if Matt and I got active in fighting the quarry, that would probably go a long way toward making people get over whatever grudge they're carrying against Matt. So we could win for ourselves, *and* help you win. Right?"

Caleb took a moment to collect his thoughts before he said, "You know we don't have a prayer, right? Have you looked at the history of gravel extraction in this province? Have you read the damned Aggregates Act? If we were all rich... if the site was a golf course instead of farmland... then we might, *might* have a prayer. But the only people in the area with any real money are the ones who sold their damned farm in the first place. And they've buggered off to Florida!" He took a breath and tried to calm down. "I mean... yeah, from your perspective, for your goals... this makes sense. And I can help out if you want. But I don't want... I don't want you to get your hopes up that we're actually going to *win* this. And, you know... if you're looking at this project as a way to distract you from something else that might be disappointing...."

"'Disappointing'? Losing my baby seems like it would be 'disappointing'? That's the best word you've got?" Caleb couldn't tell whether Sarah was angry or just amazed, but he certainly wasn't feeling a lot of appreciation for his attempt at thoughtfulness.

The smart thing to do would be to back down. Probably the kind thing too. But there was something Caleb had been wanting to say for a while, and apparently he was on some sort of speaking-his-mind roll lately. "No. I'm sorry. Of course the actual losing of the baby, that's... I don't know. Horrible. Tragic.

I get that, I do. And I've got nothing but compassion for you, seriously. I'm sorry if I sounded insensitive." But she knew he had more to say, and she wasn't accepting his apology until he was done. Sarah wasn't stupid.

He tried a smile to show that they were still friends, then said, "But... Matt said he begged you not to try again. He said he'd be happy to adopt, but you wouldn't even consider it. I don't know, maybe that's just his version, but if it's true... you need to understand, Sarah. Because of who you are and how your body's made, you're having trouble conceiving a child with the person you love. Because of who I am and the way my body's made, there's no fucking way I'm ever going to conceive a child with the person I love. Which is fine, because...." He had to laugh at himself a little. "Well, it's fine because I'm single and it's been so long since I had a date that I wonder why I even bothered coming out. But it's also fine because adoption is a good way to make a family. Hell, just finding the person you love and being with him is a good way to make a family, even without kids. You're lucky you've found Matt, and it makes me a little bit crazy to see you working so hard to get more, and maybe not appreciating how much you've already got."

He was almost done; he'd seen the tears in her eyes and was tempted to stop there, but he was pretty sure he'd gone so far that it was best to finish. "I don't mean that you shouldn't feel the pain and the loss from the miscarriages. I can't imagine how that feels, and I'm really, really sorry it happened to you. I just... it's starting to feel like you're signing yourself up for the pain, and it's all based on an idea that the only way to make a family is to give birth to it. Which I disagree with. Which I *have* to disagree with, if I ever plan to have a family of my own. You know?"

She didn't answer right away. The tears were out of her eyes now, running down her cheeks, and Caleb felt a flush of shame rising up his neck. Who the hell did he think he was, saying something like that to this woman? He'd pushed his nose in where it didn't belong, presumed on his friendship with her husband to make a comment on something that was deeply personal and totally painful for her. He'd been completely out of line, and he was getting his apology ready when Sarah stood up. He half stood as well, just an instinctive reaction to try to keep her from leaving, but she wasn't headed for the porch steps. Instead, she stepped toward him and reached out, wrapping her arms around his neck and giving him a warm hug. "I'm sorry," she whispered into his neck.

She pulled away and impatiently wiped the tears from her cheeks. "I'm sorry," she said again, her voice stronger. "I hadn't thought about it from your perspective. You know I think you're really brave, right? And I absolutely think you'll find somebody, someday, someone amazing enough to deserve to be with you. And if you decided to go for it, a baby would be *incredibly* lucky to be adopted by you and whatever perfect man you end up with. You'll make a great family. I totally believe all that; I do." Her smile wavered a little, but it held. "I'm not sure why it feels different when it comes to me and Matt. I know that it *does*, but I don't know why. But I'm going to think about it, I promise. I'm going to think about it a lot."

"I'm sorry for upsetting you."

Sarah grinned and waved impatiently at her still wet eyes. "Oh, this? Don't worry about this! I'm a sap all the time; you know that. It's even worse when I'm pregnant. You were right to say something—I think it was something I needed to hear."

This was going much more smoothly than Caleb had expected. For all that he might be impatient with Sarah's bullheadedness, he also found himself admiring her strength. Even after all the pain she'd already endured, she was keeping herself optimistic; she was still fighting for what she wanted, even against the odds. The lesson for him was pretty clear. "I'd like to help with the quarry fight," he said. "I have no idea how we're going to do it, but... yeah. We need to fight it. We need to protect the land. And help Matt. It's a good plan, Sarah."

"I'm not sure I'd call it a plan," Sarah said, her usual brightness quickly returning to her voice. "More like a faint hint of the possible beginnings of an eventual, potential idea."

"Well, it's a good one of those, then. What do we need to do to move along and make it better?"

"We need to figure it out," she said decisively, then she smiled. "Man, I wish I could have a beer."

"Come on inside and I'll steam a lemon or something, let you drink that. I'm sure it's almost as good."

"Yeah, that sounds... delicious?" But she stood up and followed Caleb inside. It felt good to be doing something, even something futile. He and Sarah might be fighting the odds, but at least they were fighting.

CHAPTER TEN

"THEY'VE got a website up," Riva reported as Peter came through the door of their motel-room office. "Looks pretty good too. Fairly factual, but lots of links to inflammatory sites that are less careful with the truth. An impassioned letter from the senior Deans explaining that their land was bought under false pretenses, a link to a page at the local elementary school where they're doing science projects on the importance of ground water, lots of pictures of happy farmers. There's even a live-feed camera—I think it must be mounted on one of the trees on the Sinclair property, near the road, panning out over the quarry site. They're calling it the 'Bearing-Witness Cam'." She nodded thoughtfully. "They either had this planned for a while, or they *really* kicked it into gear fast."

"Maybe that's why Caleb Sinclair won't return my calls," Peter said wryly. "He's been too busy with this."

"You think he's the ringleader?"

"That's what Carol Diefenbaker says." After the initial meeting between the women, Peter had stepped in. Mrs. Diefenbaker was apparently the kind of strong woman who didn't believe that other women were as capable as she was, and preferred to deal with men. "Him and the junior Mrs. Dean. Carol says she's happy to talk to us, but she's not going to cross her closest neighbor *or* the woman who taught her dyslexic grandson to read."

"Nice," Riva said, and she sounded genuine. Since she'd

become dissatisfied with her job, Riva had adopted an attitude that seemed pretty close to Peter's traditional admiration for their opponents and appreciation of the process. Peter found himself shifting to a more competitive perspective just to keep things balanced.

"Do you think it's time for phase two of our site?" he asked. They'd had a basic website up for months, but it was essentially a placeholder for the more aggressive, argument-based pages they'd put up when the time was right.

"Pretty soon," Riva said. She was still clicking at her laptop, exploring the new site. "Damn," she said, leaning forward and looking more closely at her computer. "That's nice." She looked over at Peter. "They've got an auction going on, as a fundraiser. Just online bids, it looks like. Most of it's pretty low-end stuff, but Caleb Sinclair's got a gorgeous table...."

After four days and three unreturned phone calls, Peter had been trying to get Caleb Sinclair out of his mind. But he walked across the room and peered over Riva's shoulder anyway. He couldn't help being curious. And Riva was right; the table was beautiful. It was round, with a thick pedestal base that looked like it was made of one carefully, sensually carved tree trunk. The curves were perfect, and the whole thing looked more like a graceful vase than a table. But there was a strength to the piece, as well; it didn't feel fragile or impractical.

"Wow," Peter said. "I wonder how much they're going to get for that."

Riva clicked a link at the bottom of the page. "Fifteen hundred, so far," she reported. "From somebody in Chicago." She looked over her shoulder and frowned at Peter. "Chicago. That's not great. Why is someone from so far away looking at this site?"

That was more like it—Riva back to being concerned about their progress so that Peter could simply enjoy the journey. And enjoy the fact that he knew something Riva didn't. Why was the site getting attention? "Caleb Sinclair," he responded. "I did a bit more research on him... apparently he's good. Like, *good*. He still does some midlevel work: custom cabinetry, that sort of thing. But he's having serious success with things like this, furniture that's halfway to being art. His stuff is selling as fast as he can make it, and being shipped all over the world. He's got some serious fans in Hong Kong, but the guy that sells his work says it goes to five continents."

"That could be interesting," Riva mused.

Peter nodded. It definitely could. "Before the auction, I was thinking maybe he didn't realize how useful his work could be. And, I don't know, maybe he still doesn't. The site isn't going on about how the proposed quarry is interfering with the muse of a world-renowned artist, or anything, so maybe they're still thinking small. I'd like to talk to him and try to figure him out, but the bastard won't return my calls."

"Poor Petey. Your charm didn't work on him. Does he not *understand* that the mighty Peter Carr must be loved and respected by everyone he meets?"

"It's not about my ego. It's about our opponent on this issue, not, I don't know, playing the game. He's supposed to call me back so we can negotiate and figure out solutions. He just won't play."

"Oh, he's definitely playing," Riva said, gesturing at the computer. "He's playing pretty damn well. He's just not playing according to *your* rules." She frowned a little. "And it's not like this is the first time it's happened. You've got a strategy for this, right?"

Of course this had happened before, and of course Peter had a strategy. He needed to make a few more attempts to contact the man, and then he needed to ramp up the pressure, making Caleb's refusal even to discuss the issue into a way to show how reasonable Peter was, and how hard he was trying to find a way to get along. Then he could weigh the pros and cons of inviting Caleb to some sort of public discussion. He could start the "refused to comment" notes on the website. There were lots of things he could do, dozens of strategies for dealing with someone who wasn't being part of the process.

He just didn't want to use any of those tactics on Caleb Sinclair. "I'm going to go out there," he said, trying to sound as if he was confident that it was a good idea.

Riva, of course, wasn't fooled. "Really? Why?"

"Because he won't talk to me on the phone."

"So you think it's a good idea to open the company up to accusations of harassment?"

"I'm not going to harass him."

"Continuing to pursue communication with someone who's made it crystal clear that he doesn't want to communicate with you... that doesn't sound like harassment?"

"It's business. I've received communication from someone claiming to be... well, I don't know if Trevor was saying he was Caleb's agent or an actual owner himself. Regardless, the family connection gives me a credible reason to suspect that Trevor Sinclair is acting on Caleb Sinclair's behalf, but I need to be duly diligent in ensuring that he actually is. So I need to speak with Caleb Sinclair before pursuing any further negotiations with Trevor Sinclair. That's just good business."

"You didn't make it pretty damn clear to Trevor Sinclair that you had no intention of doing business with him? You know, with your 'crush on his brother' stuff?"

"That was just... well, I don't know what the hell that was. But I'm back in the game now, and I'm shutting no doors. I'm going to go out to see Caleb Sinclair. Just once. Just to see...." Peter trailed off, and Riva's smile eased from teasing to affectionate.

"To see if this is all there is?" she suggested.

"Don't start with that," Peter said firmly. "I have a job to do, and part of the job is finding a way to make Caleb Sinclair and his team happy. It's hard to do that when I can't talk to them."

"And which of them have you *tried* talking to, other than Caleb Sinclair? Sarah Dean works during the day, I guess, but you could try to reach her once school's out."

"Maybe *you* should take that one." There was no reason for it; no excuse, even, but Peter didn't care. He thought of Riva as a coworker and teammate, but technically he was her boss, and maybe it was time he got a few perks out of that technicality. Like getting to talk to whom he wanted to talk to. "You can do that thing women do."

"Talking?" Riva guessed. "Or are we back to the tea-drinking?"

"Use your professional judgment. But don't be afraid to pull out the tea if you think it's justified." He headed for the door. "I'm going to go." Then he turned abruptly and went to one of the cheap desks he'd bought for the room, after flipping the unused mattresses up to make room. "I'll draw up some agency papers, for Trevor to represent Caleb if that's what he wants."

"Nice excuse."

"You were the one who was worried about getting the company in trouble for harassment. This is just me trying to provide a service to a prospective business associate." Peter scrolled efficiently through the files on his computer. He was sure he had a template he could adapt. "We go the extra mile, and work to truly serve the communities in which we do business." Riva's only response was a disdainful grunt. Peter found the file he was looking for and clicked to open it. Caleb Sinclair, he thought. Lover of the land, carver of the wood... master of the hounds? What was it about the man that had Peter so intrigued? And just how far was Peter going to go to satisfy his curiosity?

CHAPTER ELEVEN

IT FELT good to be back in the shop. Caleb had spent the past few days on the computer, developing the website and, when he could, working on his plans for the den he was supposed to be designing. Sarah had been great, spending her off-work hours calling everyone in town, letting them know about the campaign and drumming up donations for the fundraising auction, but she couldn't be expected to do it all.

Things were starting to come together, though, and they'd gotten a great response to their call for volunteers to be involved in the campaign. They were having a meeting at the community hall in two days to figure out who could do what; until then, they were more or less in a holding pattern. And that meant he could get back to work.

He ran his fingertips lightly over the block of wood on his work counter. It wasn't fancy or exotic, just cherry, smooth-textured and rich reddish brown, and he wished he had more of it. He'd been trying to work with local lumber as much as possible, and there was certainly a lot of cherry growing in the region. But Caleb had bought this at an estate auction, clearing the shop of a woodworker who had bought the cherry decades earlier and never gotten around to using it. The age had given the wood a richer, deeper color than fresh cherry would have, and Caleb wanted to use it for something special. He'd made the table that was currently in the auction with most of it, and now there were just a few pieces left over, odds and ends that he would have tossed into the burn pile if the wood hadn't spoken to him as it did.

He always felt a bit pompous when he had thoughts like that. As if the wood actually spoke to him. As if there were something mystical here, something more than an attractive, unusual color and a fine, even grain. It was just wood, a chunk of dead tree. But that tree had grown somewhere nearby, had absorbed nutrients from the same soil that fed the community Caleb lived in. His grandmother's garden, the beef cattle he raised, the milk from his goats and the eggs from his chickens, they all came from the same soil that had produced this tree, and that meant the tree and Caleb were related. Yeah, it was stupid, artsy nonsense that he'd never have dared to say out loud to anyone other than maybe Matt, but that didn't mean it wasn't true.

And it wasn't just Matt he'd said it to, he realized with a start. He'd said practically the same crap to The Gravel Guy when he'd visited. Jesus, what had he been thinking? And what had The Gravel Guy thought?

Maybe that was why the guy had been calling; he figured Caleb was soft in the head and would be easy to take advantage of, easy to persuade. And maybe that was why Caleb hadn't returned the calls, because he was afraid that maybe The Gravel Guy was right, and Caleb *would* be persuaded.

He tried to return to his work. He gathered all the pieces of cherry he'd saved and assembled them on the bench. Plates or bowls? Not enough big chunks, he didn't think, and the wood was maybe too simple for something that didn't have a fair bit of ornamentation itself. A small shelf, if he glued some pieces. Maybe a child-sized chair that some doting grandparent could buy to welcome a new arrival? He liked the multigenerational idea of that—it seemed like a nice tribute to the wood's history. But would the kid appreciate it, or just bang it up and spill juice on it?

"I hope I'm not interrupting." The voice broke into his

thoughts, and Caleb jumped in surprise. "Sorry!"

Caleb turned, but he didn't need his eyes to know who was in his shop. "The Gravel Guy," he said. And then wished he'd kept his mouth shut until his brain had caught up to the situation.

"I normally go by 'Peter'." The visitor was standing just inside the doorway, rubbing Diego's soft ears as the dog gazed adoringly upward. Diesel was staring at the man, his hackles up, but he hadn't growled loudly enough to warn Caleb. Maybe Caleb needed a third dog, a yappy little thing that would sound the alarm more effectively. Peter's smile was as overwhelming as ever, and Caleb reached out to the cherry on the table, trying to find something to ground himself on.

"What can I do for you?" he managed, and he was proud that he sounded almost normal.

"I saw the website. It looks good. And your table is fantastic."

"Thanks." Caleb didn't want to seem churlish, but he also didn't want to encourage this arrogant, beautiful man.

"Your brother came by," Peter said. Damn it, how had he slipped back to being "Peter"? Maybe it was stupid to cling to "The Gravel Guy," but surely Caleb could at least manage "Carr" or something more formal. But Peter was still talking, so Caleb had to abandon his train of thought. "Trevor seemed to be speaking for you, in terms of the disposition of the property. But we hadn't heard that from you, and his name's not on the deed. So I drew up these papers to authorize him to deal on your behalf, if that's what you want."

"That's not what I want." Caleb tried to swallow his anger and reminded himself that he was angry at his brother, not this man. But, no, he was angry at this man as well. "There are no deals to be made. You want a gravel pit in prime farmland; I want the exact opposite. There are no compromises, no agreements, and no deals."

"Okay," Carr said, and he lifted the papers he'd been holding and ceremonially ripped them in two. "No deals. Okay."

This seemed too easy. "So, if that's all there is...."

There was a pause, and then Peter said, "No. That's not all there is." The words seemed to mean something to him, something more than they did to Caleb, but it wasn't clear just what, and Peter's smile suggested that he didn't really expect Caleb to understand. "I...." He looked different, somehow. He looked less like a confident, brash businessman and more like a regular person. Still stunningly handsome, of course, but... he looked like Clark Kent instead of Superman. As if Caleb had needed another reason to find the man attractive.

Peter took a deep breath and looked around the shop. Caleb wasn't sure if he was genuinely curious or just looking for a distraction. "You do beautiful work," Peter said.

"Thanks. You already kind of said that. About the table."

"Yeah, sorry. I'm a bit...." Peter shrugged, then stepped forward a few steps. "Would it be okay if I hung around? Not as.... You don't want a deal. I accept that. I'm not trying to convince you of anything, I swear. I'll take the rest of the day off work. I wouldn't... if it's okay with you, I wouldn't be The Gravel Guy, not today. I... it's hard to explain, and I think I'd sound like an idiot if I tried." He stopped and frowned in thought. "Actually, I think I'd be okay with it if you thought I was an idiot. What I really don't want you to think is that I'm a scammer, that I'm trying to play you. And I'm afraid that if I tried to explain it, I'd sound like I was. Does that make sense?"

"No." It was an easy answer. But it wasn't the whole truth. "It doesn't make sense." Caleb had no idea where this was going, or what the man in front of him wanted, but he found that he didn't really care. "But if you want to stick around, I guess you can. I need to work. I guess... you're interested in woodworking? Is that it?" It sounded odd, but Caleb couldn't think of what else could be going on. And he certainly found the craft fascinating, so who was he to deny that someone else might feel the same draw? "I'm trying to find something to do with this cherry." He rested his hand on the largest block. "I *should* be drafting up some drawings for a custom den I'm working on, but the drawings don't...." He struggled for the right words. "They drain my energy. Hands-on work gives me the energy back." He stopped himself. Why the hell was he babbling on like this, as if what he was saying made sense, or as if Peter actually cared?

But Peter was smiling, and he stepped a little closer. "That's how I feel about meeting with people. Especially groups, but one on one works too, if it's the right person. Sitting around the office, reading and writing and planning... it wears me out. Then I get out where the people are, where there's ideas and emotions flying around, and it's like I suck up all the energy in the room and use it for myself."

"It's the same for me, except the exact opposite. Me being in a room like that... it's more exhausting than doing drawings."

"Well, yeah, okay, I'm not saying we're brain twins. Introvert and extrovert, I guess. I just meant... we both have good jobs for who we are, right?" And there was no way Caleb could have kept himself from returning Peter's smile, even if he'd wanted to. Peter didn't gloat about the victory, though, just took one final step closer so he could touch the chunks of wood on the table. "They remind me of a chess set, the way you've got them lined up. There's the queen, and the king, and all these little guys could be pawns." Then he stepped back and honest-to-God blushed. Caleb didn't think people could fake a blush, could they? "Sorry," Peter said. "Got a little carried away."

"No." Caleb tore his eyes away from the glorious color on Peter's cheeks, the way it stretched down into the neck of his shirt, and maybe further down below. He forced himself to look at the pieces of wood. "No, it's a good idea. They *could* be a chess set. I've never made one of those. The pawns would be easy. They just need to be turned. And the bishops, and probably the king and queen. Most of the castle would be okay, and I could just add a bit of something to the top to make it clear what it was. The knights would be tricky. I wonder...."

He was brought back to awareness of his surroundings by the scrape of wood against the concrete floor, and looked up to see Peter looking at him guiltily. "Sorry. I didn't mean to disturb you. You seemed really intent. I just...." He gestured at the stool. "I was going to sit down. Sorry."

"No, don't be sorry. It's a good idea. The chess set, I mean. I kind of zoned out there, I guess, but I think I can do it. And I've got some maple I could use for the other side. A lighter color than the cherry, but still rich and warm." Caleb reached for one of the pieces of cherry and lifted it up. "I think I can do the knights as sort of... impressionistic, or something. I'm thinking of seahorses, the way their necks are arched. I could just take that shape, not the details, just that graceful curve...." And Caleb was gone, again, lost in his imagination.

He sorted the blocks, decided which chunks would become which pieces, and then dug out the maple and did the same. He took some measurements, made a few quick sketches, and then heard an awkwardly cleared throat. Peter. Right. Just how weird was Caleb being with all this? But what did it matter? There was no reason to try to impress the guy, and Peter was the one who'd invited himself into Caleb's work space, so Caleb didn't owe him any attention. Still, the man was hard to ignore. It was a testament to how excited Caleb was about the chess set that he'd been able to go as long as he had without trying to sneak peeks. Now, he looked over and saw Peter holding his smart phone out toward Caleb.

Caleb raised an eyebrow in question, and Peter said, "I thought maybe... I found some seahorse pictures. The underside of their necks is kinda ugly, really, but I think you mean the top part, right?" He looked at Caleb for a moment longer, then slowly drew the phone back toward his chest. "Sorry. You probably already have all your ideas. You know what seahorses look like. I just got kind of caught up...."

Caleb raised his hand and stretched it toward the phone. "No. Thanks. I'm used to working alone, but... I'd like to see pictures. That'd be really...." Well, there was no point in denying it. "It's really helpful. Thank you."

"No problem." Peter handed the phone over and settled back onto his stool. Caleb glanced at his watch. He wasn't sure what time Peter had arrived, but he was pretty sure it had been at least an hour. An hour of Peter watching Caleb scurrying around like a crazed preschooler, stacking blocks of wood into different patterns and scribbling random pictures on his sketch pad. The man obviously had the patience of a saint, but that didn't mean Caleb should continue to impose on that virtue.

"This isn't what you came here for," he said.

Peter looked startled. "I guess not. I don't really know *why* I came here. I mean, I know the excuse I used, the stuff with your brother. But that's not the real reason, I don't think."

Maybe the reason Peter was so understanding of Caleb's eccentricity was because he wasn't totally balanced himself. "You don't know why you came?"

"I just really wanted to... is it going to sound insanely cheesy if I say I just wanted to see you?" Peter stood up and raked a restless hand through his perfectly styled hair. "That's probably inappropriate. A conflict of interest. I mean, I can say that I want us to get along as much as I want to, but the truth is, you are pretty strongly opposed to my employer's business plan, right? You want them to not do what they want to do. You're actively working to prevent them from being able to do it." He made a little half turn in one direction, then back the other way. It was like he was pacing, but wasn't putting the steps in the middle. "It's inappropriate for me to be pursuing something with you."

That sounded... it sounded like something that didn't make any sense. "'Pursuing something'? What exactly do you think you're pursuing?"

Another startled look. "I don't know. I mean... you know.

You're interesting. Attractive. I'm interested and attracted. So I guess I'd be pursuing... you."

Caleb's hands returned to the comforting warmth of the cherry blocks, but he forced himself not to turn his eyes away from Peter's face. "But that would be inappropriate," he prompted, tentative but intrigued.

"Yeah, it would," Peter agreed. He kept his eyes locked on Caleb's. "But I'm beginning to think I don't really care."

CHAPTER TWELVE

IT WAS not a good sign that Caleb's flustered expression made Peter want to wrap him up in blankets and cuddle him until he was back to himself. Or else kiss him until he forgot what he'd been flustered about. Neither response was professionally appropriate, and neither was in keeping with Peter's past behavior. He was usually impatient with people who lost their poise. And if he was going to overlook that flaw, which seemed only fair, considering how ridiculously he himself was behaving, then he shouldn't want to waste time with cuddling and kissing; he should be craving full-body nakedness, as soon as possible. This whole thing was out of control, and he was being an idiot.

Then Caleb smiled at him, tentative but curious, and Peter stopped giving a damn about what he should be doing. "Do you want to take a break?" he suggested. "I mean... it's been interesting watching you work. And if you need to keep going, that's fine; I understand. Just because I took some time off doesn't mean the rest of the world has to. But if you wanted to talk for a bit...."

"Do you want to go outside?" Caleb suggested. He gestured toward one of the huge windows that let natural light into the workshop. "It's a nice day."

"Sure," Peter agreed. Outside, inside, whatever. He felt almost dizzy. Not physically, but as though his emotional world had been spun around and was now having trouble figuring out which way was up.

He fell in behind Caleb as they headed for the shop door. There was a garage door that must be useful for getting large projects in and out, but they headed through the regular-sized opening beside it. The dogs trailed behind them, and Peter wondered when Diesel had stopped staring at him like he was dinner. He'd been so wrapped up in Caleb that he'd barely noticed the dog. "That's a great shop," he said. "Well designed. Functional." He had no idea why he was saying any of that, but Caleb didn't seem to mind.

"Thanks. I put a lot of thought into it."

They stood awkwardly for a moment just outside the shop door. "We could go for a walk," Caleb said, "but you've already wiped out in the mud once. And it was probably pretty hard on your shoes too."

"Yeah, sorry. I'm not really dressed for the outdoors." Peter's work uniform of a conservative suit and Italian shoes made sense most of the time, but in Caleb's world it seemed absurd. And again, Peter just didn't care. "Maybe we could sit on the porch?"

"Yeah, okay." They started in that direction, and then Caleb stopped so abruptly that Peter almost ran into him. Caleb turned and looked searchingly into Peter's eyes. Peter had no idea what Caleb was looking for, but he tried to return the gaze as honestly as he could. "Is this... I should just make it clear that there is no fucking way I am selling this land," Caleb said. "And there is no way I am backing down from fighting the quarry. No chance of that happening. I should make that clear."

"Yeah. Okay." Peter tried a smile. "And I have no power to change my company's mind about any of the significant aspects of this project. I can suggest modifications, or ways to make things go more smoothly, but in terms of the large-scale decisions, I don't get a voice. There is absolutely nothing I can do to stop this quarry. I sympathize with your objections, and if you want to set up an appointment to discuss any concerns...

well, I think I'd ask Riva to handle that, if it's okay with you. I already tried to pass you off to her once, but it didn't really take. I just...." He didn't want to sound like a little boy, but he couldn't think of any other way to express what he wanted to say. "I just hope we can get to know each other as *us*, without all that getting in the way. That's what I'd like. If it's okay with you."

Caleb's nod took a while to get started, but once it was going, it seemed sincere. "Yeah. That sounds okay."

Not the most enthusiastic acceptance Peter had ever heard, but he'd take it. And with that adorable, shy look on Caleb's face, Peter was inspired to try to take a little more. He moved slowly, carefully, bringing his hand up to Caleb's arm, then his shoulder, then his neck. Somewhere around the shoulder Peter could see Caleb realize what was happening, his eyes widening, shifting just a little, and then returning to Peter's in acceptance of the suggestion. Peter leaned down a little, Caleb stretched up, and their lips met.

It was simple, and sweet. No explosions of passion, just a quiet exchange of breaths. A symbol of intent rather than the full execution of a scheme. It was all Peter needed, at least for the time being, and apparently Caleb felt the same way, because he shifted away before Peter did. It didn't feel like a rejection, though, especially when Peter saw Caleb's smile.

And that was when Peter's cell phone rang. He wished he hadn't programmed different ringtones in, because he really didn't need to know that it was the main office calling. Any other call he'd have ignored, but this one he needed to answer. He made a face at Caleb. "Sorry," he started to say, but Caleb just waved a hand.

"Take it," he said with another sweet smile. "I'm going to go get a drink. You want something? A beer, or water?"

"Yeah, a beer'd be great. If I'm taking a day off, I should definitely have an afternoon drink. Thanks." Peter stepped back a few steps and answered his phone as he watched Caleb heading for the house. "Peter Carr."

"Peter, it's Barbara."

Damn. The CEO. She and Peter were friendly enough, but she wasn't his normal contact person. "Barbara, hi. What's up?"

"What are you up to down there, Peter?" She didn't sound accusatory, but he had a sudden flash of paranoia, wondering whether his phone was rigged to broadcast his conversations to the head office or something. But that was stupid, and there was nothing wrong with what he was doing with Caleb Sinclair, anyway. Probably.

"Uh—do you want a full report, or is there something specific you're interested in?"

"Mostly I'm interested in finding out why Jayne fucking Blythe is calling the office to let us know she is throwing the full weight of her celebrity behind the quarry opposition."

"Jayne Blythe? The singer?"

"The legend, Peter. She may not be doing much lately, but she's one of Canada's biggest stars, ever. Why the fuck is she interested in a damned quarry?"

"She doesn't live around here. Not unless she owns property under an assumed name, or something. We checked for big-name locals."

"She tweets, Peter. You know how I feel about the damned tweets."

"I feel the same way, Barbara. Has someone spoken to her? If she's in the area, I can go over and see her, try to figure out what's going on."

"You're damned right you can see her. She's in Toronto, and she's agreed to meet us at the office at nine tomorrow morning. I want you here. And I want you to knock her socks off. Shut her up. Whatever. I do *not* want us to be the company that pissed off the Northern Nightingale."

"Of course. I'll be there. I'll bring Riva too; she's great at the technical side of things."

"You can bring the Toronto Symphony Orchestra if you think it'll help. I want this resolved, Peter."

"Absolutely. I'm on it." He heard the phone disconnect at the other end, and lowered the phone from his ear. Shit. He turned and saw Caleb stepping off the bottom stair, two dogs trailing behind him, two beers held in one hand. Damn it. Peter wanted to stay. He wanted to sit on those porch steps with Caleb and sip his beer and look out at the forest when he wasn't looking at Caleb, and he wanted to figure out just what he'd found in this man.

But he couldn't do it, and he could see the moment Caleb read that truth on his face. "You need to head out?" Caleb asked, his voice light and casual.

"Yeah, I do. Trouble at work." And that was a bit awkward, because in a work sense, Peter's losses were Caleb's victories. But Peter wasn't ready to acknowledge this as a loss, not yet. It was just a challenge. That was how he was supposed to be thinking.

"Okay."

Peter had no idea if Caleb was actually feeling as casual as he sounded, or if this was a façade. And if it *was* a false front, what was Caleb covering behind it, exactly?

"I don't want to. I want to stay here."

"But you have to go. I get it." And there it was, the tight smile that let Peter know all the rest of it was an act as well.

"Fuck!" Peter could tell that Caleb was taken aback by that little explosion, but hopefully that was good. Let Caleb realize that Peter was upset about this too. "Something's gone weird. I have to go and deal with it. It's my job; it's what I do."

"I heard you the first several times you said that."

"Yeah. But you're pissed off anyway."

"No, I'm not pissed off. You have to go. It's your job. I get it. I'm not happy about it, but I understand. Those farms aren't going to destroy themselves, after all."

Well, that shouldn't have been unexpected, and Peter shouldn't let it sting. He shook his head, then frowned at Caleb. "You don't happen to know Jayne Blythe, do you?"

"The singer? I wouldn't say I know her... we're not friends or anything. But she's bought some pieces from me, yeah. Why?"

For the life of him, Peter would swear that Caleb was genuinely, innocently curious about the reason for Peter's question. Damn it. "Just... work. I have to go. I... look, if I give you a call sometime, is there any chance that maybe you'd pick up, or at least return the call? Like I said, I'll ask Riva to take over all business communication with you. So if I call, it's just *me* calling. Would you pick up if it was just me?"

"Does that person even exist, Peter? The *you* that isn't all tied up in your work? You said it's your job and it's what you do. But it's who you are too, isn't it? I'm not saying it in a critical way; remember, you said we've both found jobs that are perfect for us. It's a perfect fit for you, and that means... it means you're perfectly fitted to ruining my home. I think... if things were different, if we'd met some other way, I'd be picking up the phone, absolutely. But as things are... I don't think it's a good idea."

Peter didn't want to accept that. He wanted to argue, and negotiate, and persuade, and use all the skills that made him so good at his job to allow him to be good at this too. He wanted to be good at having a life. But maybe Caleb was right. Maybe there was just no way this was going to work. "Would you... can you think about it? Will you pick up the phone at least to talk, even if you end up hanging up twenty seconds later?"

Caleb thought about it, then nodded slowly. "Yeah. I can think about it. I'll... I'll probably pick up, just to talk."

That was as much of a commitment as Peter should try for, he decided. "Okay. I have to go. But I'll give you a call, okay? In a couple days, maybe."

"Okay." Caleb's fingers were rubbing Diego's ears absently, and Diesel seemed to have picked up on the fact that Peter was no longer quite as popular with the pack leader as he had been moments before. The larger dog was watching Peter a little more closely than Peter would have liked, and he decided it was a good time to get the hell out of there.

"A couple days," he repeated, and then he headed for the car. He was behind the wheel and halfway down the driveway when Riva picked up his call. "Riva, have a look at Caleb Sinclair's woodworking website and see if he's got links to the quarry site. And see if you can get your hands on his full client list. Things are getting interesting."

CHAPTER THIRTEEN

CALEB watched the car disappear down his driveway and looked down at the bottles in his hand. At least he hadn't twisted the caps off yet. So, a waste of his time and energy, but not a waste of perfectly good beer.

He tried to laugh it off. He'd been wrapped up in the excitement of creating something from the cherry, and he'd let his enthusiasm spill over into something it shouldn't have. That was all. A short conversation, a quick kiss. Nothing, really. Just a silly little incident, barely even worthy of an anecdote.

He resolutely ignored the churning emptiness in his gut, returned to the kitchen to drop off the beer, and looked over toward his laptop. He could look up his *own* seahorse pictures. It wasn't like Google was hard to use. Peter's gesture hadn't been considerate; it had been pretty insulting, really, like he thought Caleb couldn't do something that basic on his own. *Ooh, thank you, Gravel Guy, for giving me this wonderful gift of images! What would I have done without you? Sure, Gravel Guy, destroy my farm; that'd be super! I don't need a home, as long as I have you and your wonderful pictures of sea creatures!*

The phone call had been a blessing. He jiggled the mouse to wake up the laptop and waited for the search screen to appear. Was the bottom of a seahorse's neck ugly? He'd soon find out. The browser opened on the e-mail page that he and Sarah had set up for their anti-quarry project, and as he moved the cursor up to type in his search terms, he froze.

Three hundred and twenty new messages. That didn't make sense. That couldn't be right. Had Sarah set up a program so each student at the school sent an e-mail?

He clicked to open the first message. It was from someone in British Columbia, sending her support. That was odd, but kind of nice. He had no idea how she'd found the site, but it was great to read her thoughts. He'd have to answer that one, for sure.

He returned to the inbox, and found that four new messages had arrived since he'd gone to read the first. He clicked one of those, and checked the signature line at the bottom. Guyana? He wasn't... was that in Africa, or South America? He really should know that, but more importantly, why the hell was someone in Guyana reading about their quarry, and sending an e-mail in support?

He checked his watch and found his phone. When he heard the familiar voice, he said, "Sarah? Have you checked the website? There's... something's going on."

"I was just going to call you!" She sounded excited, happy, and Caleb decided that no matter the outcome, the project was worth it just to have put that tone in her voice. "We're all over! We've gone viral, or something! I just got off the phone with the service provider; we have to upgrade our package because we're getting so many hits. And have you seen the prices on the auction items? Your table's up over five grand, but even the crappy stuff is getting big bids. Caleb, this is working!"

Well, he didn't want her to get carried away. "We need more than just money and attention, though. We need... damn, I don't know, we need pressure. Results." It hurt to say it, but he did it anyway. "We need our own Gravel Guy."

"What?"

Oh. He should probably keep some things to himself. "Peter Carr. An expert at making things... I don't know, someone who knows who to talk to, who to pressure. We should call those environmental groups, the ones we sent the press release to. We should see if they can recommend someone who could represent us. We can't afford a full-time person, but it would be a good idea to pay for a few hours of direction, helping us to get a strategy. I mean, we've got the ball rolling, somehow. But now we need to make sure it's rolling in the right direction, you know?"

"Brilliant idea, babe. We need a consultant. We need Anti-Gravel Guy."

"Or Anti-Gravel Girl."

"Fair enough. Okay, who are we going to call for recommendations?"

It was fun to strategize, and to have an ally. And it was a distraction, which was wonderful, because Caleb really didn't want any time to let his mind wander. They stayed on the phone for almost an hour, going over the e-mails and comments on the website, counting their Facebook "likes," and trying to figure out what had set it all in motion.

When Caleb finally got off the phone, he had twelve voice mails waiting. Some were from earlier in the day, when he'd been out in the shop; the phone was a distraction, and he didn't usually take it out with him. Most of the calls were from locals wanting to know what the next step was, but a couple were from people he'd sold work to, intrigued by the link he'd added to his website. And there it was, among all the rest, the low alto voice he'd grown up hearing on his grandparents' record player.

"Caleb, darling, it's Jayne Blythe. I was on your site, looking to see what new treats you had for me, and I came across the link to that horrible quarry! It must be so terrible for you, to have them even *talking* about something like that being put in next door. An artist needs a peaceful environment, darling! I've decided to make this my next project. I'm going to let *everyone* know. I've set up a meeting with those corporate bloodsuckers to give them a piece of my mind! I'll call you tomorrow to let you know how things went."

Well. That explained quite a bit, really. Caleb thought of the pained look on Peter's face when he'd gotten the call, and wondered who it had been from. Just Riva, his local partner, or someone further up the hierarchy at the company headquarters? It should be funny. The Gravel Guy, full of smooth urban confidence, flustered by a geriatric singer's need for a hobby. It *was* funny.

Caleb looked down at the dogs sprawled at his feet and nudged each of them with his toes. "Funny, huh, guys?" Diego at least had the courtesy to wag his tail, but Diesel just looked up at Caleb. The damn dog only had two expressions; he was either fiercely, aggressively intent, or he looked horribly sad. And this time, lying there under the table and being softly kicked by his master, was one of the sad times.

"Oh, shut up, Diesel. It's funny." The dog's ears pricked forward, and for a moment, Caleb thought he'd convinced the creature, but then the dog growled and sprang to his feet. Diego stumbled upright a little more slowly and much less gracefully, but he was, as always, willing to follow his brother. Diesel was staring at the back door, and the low rumble from his throat didn't stop until Trevor's head appeared in the glass window.

The door opened and Trevor strode inside as if, indeed, he owned the place. "Hey, guys!" he said cheerfully. He bent to greet Diego while Diesel settled back into his spot at Caleb's feet. "I thought I'd come by for dinner."

"What are you making?" Caleb tried, but he only earned a blank look from Trevor. Something pushed him to try again. "Did you pick up takeout?"

"Jesus, Caleb." Trevor looked disappointed. "It's nice that you have money, okay? I'm sure that's great for you. But could you maybe be a bit less of an asshole about it when somebody else doesn't?"

"Did you call Mr. Taylor about that job?"

"Yeah." Trevor sounded disgusted. "I went by to see him, even. There were, like, fifteen high-school kids working in the store. He wants them young and dumb enough to not know when they're being taken advantage of. Minimum wage, and he treats them like slaves, I bet."

"Minimum wage is better than *no* wage, Trevor. And he told me that was just to start. He said he likes to promote from within. And if everyone else is a high-school kid, then they can't work full-time, so you'd have an edge."

"Do you even know how patronizing you sound? Giving me a fucking pep talk for a bullshit job that I could do in my sleep?"

"Well, that'd be an extra bonus, then. If you could do the job in your sleep, you wouldn't have to pay for an apartment, because you could sleep on the job." Apparently Caleb's attempted levity wasn't appreciated, because his brother just scowled.

Then he brightened. "I heard your auction is really taking off. Over five grand for that table? Jesus, Caleb, I didn't know there were people stupid enough to pay that much! I think there's some serious potential, here. I'll take care of the sales and distribution, and I can help with the carpentry too, if we need. You can hire a few kids to... I don't know. You could just make a template, right? And then the kids could glue shit together, and saw it up.... We could get one of those computer laser saw things, that does all the cutting for you. One kid does sandpaper, one does stain, one assembles, and we could probably do a couple tables an hour, right? Ten grand an *hour*, Caleb. That's the kind of opportunity I've been looking for."

Caleb sighed. "It doesn't work that way, Trevor. People are paying for the craftsmanship, and they're paying for something unique. If they want something mass-produced and slapped together, they'll go pay a hundred bucks at Ikea and assemble it themselves."

"But they're buying on the *Internet*, Caleb. They can't tell what the craftsmanship is until it gets to them. And by the time they realize it's not unique, it'll be too late."

"Then they'll return it."

"Well, so you change that. Make all sales final."

"I'm not interested in tricking my customers, Trevor. I produce unique, handcrafted pieces. That's what I do, and what I want to keep doing."

Trevor looked hurt. "Why are you... why is it so *important* to you that I not succeed? I mean, you'll turn down a huge opportunity for yourself, just because it would be an opportunity for me too? Really? Why? We're the only ones left, Caleb. From our whole family, from all those generations that you seem so fucking attached to, there's just you and me left. So why do you want me to suffer?"

"Oh, for Christ's sake...." But Caleb had no idea where to even begin, and he was pretty sure there was no point anyway. He pushed his chair back so impatiently that Diego scrambled to his feet in alarm. "Sorry, buddy," Caleb muttered, and the dog wagged his tail forgivingly. Caleb looked over at Trevor. "I'll make dinner," he said. "You want a chicken stir-fry?"

"How about beef?" Trevor suggested, his dramatic outrage apparently forgotten. "I think I need more red meat in my diet."

"Fine," Caleb agreed. He didn't really care, and with Trevor, it was almost always easiest to just go along.

CHAPTER FOURTEEN

PETER spent that night and most of the next day scrambling to make up lost ground. He'd been overconfident, and was caught flat-footed when he should have been poised and ready in the starter's blocks. He'd let himself get distracted.

But the meeting with Jayne Blythe had gone well. After a rocky start, Peter had been able to use his charm, and Riva's strong arguments, to explain how the province needed gravel. He'd admired Ms. Blythe's generous work in raising money for the new wing of the children's hospital, and pointed out the many tons of gravel that had been needed for the construction there. He'd talked about global warming and fossil fuels and shown the amount of oil that would be burned if they tried to ship gravel from way up north. And wasn't she from Northern Ontario, herself? She must not appreciate the way these southerners referred to the north as if it were some sort of wasteland, good only for supplying the rapacious southern cities with raw materials.

He'd walked out of the meeting, his arms still warm from the hug he'd exchanged with the Northern Nightingale, and everything had been right with his world. It was like a drug, the rush he got from talking to people—persuading them, winning them over. His whole body felt alive; hell, he was a little bit turned on.

But thinking about sex led to thinking about Caleb, and then the rush was gone. The glow of achievement dimmed and faded away as he thought about Caleb's quiet intensity, his innocent enthusiasm for his seahorse chess set... his sweet, simple kiss. Damn it. Peter had seen the movies; a new romantic interest was supposed to make you feel good, not bad. What was the point of any of it if it didn't make him happy?

But he remembered that short time in Caleb's shop, and didn't think *unhappy* was the right word to describe his feelings then. Not at all. It had been a different sort of happiness, maybe; a calm, peaceful feeling instead of the jittery thrill he got from his job. Maybe he was being greedy, thinking he could have both sorts of joy. Certainly he was being incredibly optimistic, at least in this situation.

Because Caleb was going to be pissed. Getting Jayne Blythe on board had been a huge achievement. If things had gone badly enough, if the locals had been able to take the publicity Blythe had given them and they'd used it properly, they might actually have won this thing. Peter's company wasn't a one-trick pony, with only the gravel quarry to worry about. They were big, with their fingers in a lot of different pies, and they wanted a positive public image. Needed it, for some of their more consumer-sensitive endeavors. Sure, those were all run under different corporate names, with positive advertising and all the rest, but if the publicity for the parent corporation got bad enough, it would affect the whole group. Nobody was going to want to buy their snacks from the Daybreak Bakery line if they hated Daybreak's parent company for its gravel-extraction activities. The quarry site had been chosen not only because there was available land and a rich vein of aggregates; it had also been chosen because nobody in the area seemed likely to be able to form a strong defense to the pit.

Caleb Sinclair. Peter had to smile. Even if it had been mostly accidental, the man had almost done it. He'd surprised them. Surprised Peter. It was impressive, but it had just been good luck. Once Peter had gotten his head back in the game, he'd taken care of things, and now everyone was happy again. Barbara had practically hugged him on her way out of the boardroom, and was now, he was pretty sure, taking the whole thing as a positive, since she'd been given the chance to meet a Canadian music legend.

Yeah, it was all going well, again, just as it should be. Riva had stopped by her office to pick up a few things, and then the two of them would be heading back down to their dingy motel in Rocky Creek to get back in the game. They'd release their second-wave website, they'd make nice with the locals, and they'd sit back and watch as the first scoop full of dirt lifted off the farmland.

And then Peter imagined Caleb standing on his hilly farm, sadly watching the excavation. Damn it. He pushed the idea out of his mind and strode down the hallway. "Riva?" he called when he neared her office. "You ready to go?"

She popped her head into the hallway. "I need an hour," she said. No explanation, no excuse.

"What for?"

"For me." She looked as if she was thinking about testing that and seeing if it was enough to make Peter back off, but then she sighed and added, "And for my fiancé, who thinks it would be nice if we could at least see each other face-to-face, considering that I'm back in town after more than a week away and am planning to be away for more than another week."

"Oh." They'd driven up that morning, not the night before, so, yeah, Riva hadn't had time to take care of any personal stuff. "Okay. Just an hour?"

"Possibly two," she decided. "We were thinking of lunch."

"I'd be thinking of a hotel room, if I were you." He grinned. "But I'm not. So, yeah, enjoy your lunch. I can find ways to entertain myself. Or, you know, *do work*, since it's the middle of the morning on a weekday."

"Don't even try, Peter. How long were you goofing off yesterday out at the Sinclair place?" She smiled with the contented look of someone who knows she's won. "Actually, I think maybe three hours. Three hours should do it."

"Okay, stop talking before this turns into an overnight getaway! You want me to pick you up somewhere? In three hours?"

"No. I want you to give me the car keys, and I'll pick *you* up. In three and a half hours."

"Riva...." He tried to make his voice growly and warning, like Caleb's when he'd ordered the big dog to back off, but it obviously didn't work, because Riva just smiled at him.

"Great. So, the keys are...."

He fished the keys out his pocket. "That's *my* car, Riva. Not a rental."

"It's not like I haven't driven it before." She pocketed the keys and ran her hands down her slim figure, straightening her suit. She gave him a quick, almost shy look and asked, "Do I look okay?"

That was easy to answer. "You look beautiful. Scott's a lucky guy."

"Yeah," she agreed, and then she headed down the hall.

Peter's phone rang on his way to his own office, and he answered it only to be greeted with an abrasive female voice practically shouting, "Petey Carr! The little engine that could!"

Jesus Christ. Peter did not need this right now. He ducked inside his office door. "Penny?"

"Petey! Good to hear from you!"

"You called *me*, Penny."

"Yes I did! And I have a reason for it too. Want to hear?"

"I guess I'd better."

"Penelope Mund-Fischer and Associates is going to be doing some work in your neck of the woods. Down in Rocky Creek,

Ontario! I'll tell you, Peter, I have no fucking idea where that is, so my GPS had better not let me down. I just thought I'd call in early and say 'hi'; let you know I'm on my way. It sounds like a pretty small place, so I'm sure I'll run into you."

Oh, no. "They hired you? The anti-quarry guys?"

"Believe me, that is one of the first things we're going to have to change! 'Anti-quarry guys' really doesn't have a great ring to it, you know? I'm thinking 'Farmland Crusaders' or something like that... we'll have to set up a focus group and see what flies." Penny sounded like she was having a great time, and she probably was. She had a totally different style than Peter, but they both loved their jobs, and they were both damned good at them.

"How'd they find you?" He wasn't sure he wanted to know.

"They asked around. I'd actually been thinking about giving them a call, offering my services... the Northern Nightingale has got some powerful friends, you know, and God bless the tweetosphere. But they came to me, which is always nice. Easier to negotiate rates from a position of strength, and all that."

Peter bit back any Northern-Nightingale-related responses. He didn't think he wanted Jayne's change of heart to be publicized just yet. He also tried not to worry about how much Caleb and his friends were paying Penny. She was a professional, but that didn't mean she wouldn't charge as much as she thought she could get away with. But that was none of his business. "Well, that's great, Penny. It's always fun to work with you, and I think you'll really like the folks down there. And you know, if they're a little low on cash, they can probably pay you in eggs or something."

"They can pay me in tables, from the looks of things. You seen the prices on that auction lately?"

Stupid, beautiful table. "Not lately, no. But I'm glad you'll be taken care of. When are you getting into town? You'll need a bit of time to get things sorted out, but we should definitely set up a meeting."

"I'm on my way now. Just got off the plane, and I'm standing in line for my rental."

Great. Maybe he could get her to pick him up as she passed, and they could carpool. "Okay, then. Maybe sometime tomorrow we should meet?"

"I'll keep that option in mind, Petey, but I'm going to have to consult with my clients first, and see how they want to proceed."

He almost smiled at her smug tone; her assumption that the locals would be easily cowed and would agree with whatever she said. He didn't think it was going to be quite that simple. Then again, they'd been smart enough to hire an expert, so they'd probably be smart enough to listen to her. "Okay, well, give me a call if you want to set something up."

"I don't think I'll need to call... from what I've heard, I'll just bang on the wall! You're staying at the motel, right?"

He sighed. "Yeah. You too?"

"Of course! So I'm sure I'll see you there! Talk to you later, Petey!"

And the line went mercifully dead. Peter only hesitated for a moment before hitting the buttons to call Riva.

"Peter?"

"They hired Penelope Mudfucker."

"They didn't."

"They did."

"Shit." There was only a brief pause, and then Riva said, "Two hours. Okay? Two hours."

"Yeah, okay. I'll be waiting for you downstairs." There was nothing more to say. Penny Mund-Fischer. Damn. She was annoying, but she was excellent at her job. Peter felt the smile growing from inside and reaching his lips. This was going to be good.

Chapter Fifteen

Caleb felt like a total fraud, sitting there at the big table in the mayor's dining room. Everyone else at the meeting was some sort of solid citizen: the doctor and his school-teacher wife; the owner of the hardware store; a couple of well-respected farmers; the mayor herself... and Caleb Sinclair, son of a drunk and brother of a druggie, near high-school-dropout, and, of course, well-known homosexual. It was a sign of Penny Mund-Fischer's professionalism that she hadn't blinked an eye when they'd been introduced. Well, professionalism or ignorance, he supposed; maybe she just hadn't been in town long enough to figure out who everyone was.

He hadn't had much to say during the meeting, but he'd listened closely and taken a lot of notes. So maybe that could be how he'd contribute; he'd record other people's good ideas. It wasn't exciting, but it was something.

"So I'll draft another press release," Penny said, nodding at the assemblage. "And we've all got our jobs for the direct contacts—remember, these are politicians, so they're used to saying a lot without committing to anything. They need to be pushed a little. If they say they'll look into it, you ask what information they'd like you to send them, and when they'll get back to you about it. Write it all down, and we'll make follow-up calls at the appropriate times. Caleb," she said, and he actually jumped a little, "I'd like you to keep working on your client list. International attention doesn't translate directly to votes, but it definitely comes across as pressure, especially if you can drum up any more celebrities. And the regional customers are great; they've got money *and* votes, and that's a good combination."

"I don't...." Caleb stopped, and wished he hadn't started. But Penny smiled at him encouragingly, and Sarah and Matt were there, too, so he forced himself to keep going. "I don't really think people are going to care too much. I mean, I built their cabinetry, or I made them a desk or something. I don't think they really care about my opinion on saving farmland." He saw Penny's concerned frown and hastened to add, "I'll call them! I'll do what I can. I just, you know... I don't want to get anyone's hopes up."

"Every little bit helps," Penny said smoothly. Then she asked, "Have you heard back from Jayne Blythe yet? She was supposed to call you yesterday after her meeting, wasn't she?"

"Yeah, she was." Caleb didn't want to say it. "But I think she was meeting with... with Peter Carr. I expect he did what he does, and she loves him now, and we've gotten all we're going to out of her."

"Even if that's true, we still got a lot." Penny seemed philosophical about it all. "And you're right, Peter *is* very persuasive. But I'd like you to follow up with Ms. Blythe just the same. You say you don't have her phone number, but you can e-mail her, right?"

"Yeah. I can. I will." God, this was worse than sales, and Caleb *hated* sales. But he thought of the fragile winter wheat, its shoots fresh and green in the fields that were about to be lost, and he nodded. "I will," he said with more determination.

"Great." Penny rewarded him with a smile, her sleek silver hair bobbing as she nodded. "Okay, then, I think we've all got our jobs. I'll be here for another couple days, and then I'll be in Toronto talking to politicians, and after that I'll work remotely for a while. Sound good?"

It sounded fine. It wasn't like they could afford to pay someone like this to work for them full-time.

After the meeting broke up, Caleb walked outside with Sarah and Matt. He didn't bother to ask about Sarah's pregnancy; he'd been spending so much time with her, he knew he would have noticed if she was dealing with another miscarriage. Maybe this had been the key all along: Sarah could carry babies to term as long as she was passionately involved in a fight for farmland preservation. It made as much sense as any other theory he'd heard, but he still quietly knocked on the wooden porch rail as they passed.

"You okay to contact her, Caleb?" Matt was watching him sympathetically. "Jayne Blythe? I know you hate that stuff."

"I hate having huge pits dug next door to my house too," he said. "So, lesser of two evils, I guess."

"Are there any other celebrities on your client list?" Sarah sounded like she was half teasing, half serious. "I still can't believe you didn't tell us that Jayne Blythe bought your work!"

"She's the biggest name," Caleb said. "I just figured, you know... it's not like she's my friend, or anything. She just saw something that caught her eye."

"After a certain point, modesty is silly," Sarah insisted. "You're a carpentry star! Admit it."

"So, do I get a reality show out of this?" Caleb smiled awkwardly and stepped away to let them know the conversation was over. "I've got calls to make. I'll see you guys... I don't know; tomorrow, probably."

They separated, and Caleb climbed into his truck and pulled his phone out of the glove box. He only had one missed call, but the message left was a doozy.

"Hey, Caleb, it's Peter. I hope you're just busy, and not screening my call. Look, this is an awkward situation, and it probably doesn't make sense for us to pursue anything. Not right now, at least. But I'd still like us to be friends, if that's at all possible. I mean... I like you, and once you get over the part where you hate me and everything I stand for, I think you like me too."

The warm laughter in Peter's voice did something unusual and quite pleasant to Caleb's lower abdomen. *"And I'm not going to be on this project forever, and Toronto isn't all that far away, if you wanted to.... Okay, I'm getting ahead of myself, obviously. But I thought maybe we could... I don't know, I was thinking dinner? Somewhere else. We could drive up to London, if you wanted, and try to get to know each other in a neutral setting. I know you're busy, and I know you've got a lot on your mind. But if you can find time, I'd like it a lot. Give me a call."*

Caleb had no idea how he felt. Well, no, he had some idea. He felt nervous, and excited, and a little bit queasy—but in a good way. What he really had no idea about was what he wanted to do. What he *should* do. He wanted to be smart, didn't want to sign up for heartache... but he really, really wanted to hear Peter's laugh again.

He sighed, and sat there in his truck on one of Rocky Creek's few residential streets, and scrolled through his contacts until he found the number he wanted: the one he'd denied having when asked about it earlier. He had no idea what to do about Peter, but he knew what to do about someone else. When the familiar voice answered, he said, "Ms. Blythe? It's Caleb Sinclair. I'm really sorry to bother you, and I'm sure you don't want to get dragged into anything, but I was wondering... would you be interested in coming down to see my workshop? I have some new pieces that aren't up for sale yet, and I think you might like some of them." Because he didn't want to be sneaky, and because he knew she knew anyway, he added, "While you're here, I'd love it if you could take a walk with me, and have a look at the land they want to build the quarry on. I don't know if you like wildflowers, but the bloodroot is out. And the leeks too, if you like wild leeks." Damn it. He'd started pretty strong, at least for him, but now he was babbling. He forced himself to stop speaking.

"Caleb...." She sounded cautious, and he braced himself for her refusal. But after a pause, she said, "I love wild leeks. And I'd love to see your new work. But I can't promise anything. I should have called you back after my meeting the other day, but... I had a lot to think about. I don't want to be a hypocrite, and we *do* need gravel."

"I know we do. I don't want to be a hypocrite, either. I understand if you can't make it. Or if you want to come see the shop, and not talk about the quarry. I'd be honored to have you visit, no strings attached."

He heard her sigh. "You really are such a lovely young man. Have you met Peter Carr? Different from you, but, really... another lovely young man."

"I've met him, yes." And Caleb had to smile. "You're right. He is lovely. But he's also a smooth, smooth talker, and I'd really like you to see the property for yourself rather than just hear about it from him."

"Well, that seems fair." The smile in her voice carried over the phone line. "I accept your invitation. And the advantage of being retired is that I can make my own schedule. Would you be available, say... the day after tomorrow? I could arrive in time for a quick tour of your shop, and then we could have lunch and go for a walk?"

"That sounds great. Thank you."

"Thank you, Caleb. I look forward to seeing your work." And then she was gone, and Caleb let his head fall back against the seat. What the hell was he doing? And what was he going to give the Northern fucking Nightingale for lunch?

But those were details, and he was on a roll. He found another number, and was almost painfully relieved when he got voice mail instead of a real person. He could only handle so much communicating in one evening. "Peter, it's Caleb. Dinner sounds like a terrible idea, but I'm in anyway. How about tomorrow night? Give me a call."

He ended the call and dropped the phone onto the seat next to him. He felt like he'd been temporarily possessed, but the calls had exorcised him. Then he thought about the task he'd been assigned at the meeting. He had to go through his entire client list and make phone calls just as painful as those, over and over again. What the hell had he gotten himself into?

CHAPTER SIXTEEN

WHEN Peter showed up at Caleb's house the next night, Diesel gave him a dirty, dirty look, but didn't growl at all, and Peter considered it a huge victory. He bounced up on the porch steps, buoyed by his pet-charming ways, and glanced down midair to realize where his foot was going to land. There was no way to fix it, no time, but he did what he could, and managed to throw himself a bit to one side so only half of his weight landed on Diego's outstretched tail.

Even half the weight of someone Peter's size was quite a bit, and Diego yelped and jerked away with a terrified backward glance. Diesel rushed over, hackles up, growl deep and threatening. "Shit! Sorry! Sorry, Diego, sorry, Diesel...."

The door opened then, of course, and Caleb was there, almost certainly wondering why Peter had chosen to attack the pets.

"I stepped on Diego," Peter said quickly. "I'm so sorry!"

"His tail?" Caleb glanced at the dog. "You okay, buddy?" The dog's tail wagging apparently reassured his master. "Don't worry about it; I do it about five times a day. I swear, it's like he shoves his tail under your feet on purpose. I think he wants the attention."

"I kind of... I kind of *jumped* on him...."

"What? Why?"

Two excellent questions. "I was just coming up the steps, you know. Energetically. And then, there he was."

"He seems fine." Caleb crouched down and ran his hand quickly and firmly down the dog's tail. It wasn't easy to do, considering how vigorously the tail was wagging, and the movement made Peter feel better. "You're okay, right, buddy?" Caleb asked, and the dog licked his face in reply. "Yeah, that's what I thought. Stop trying to trip people." He straightened and opened the door to the house. "Inside, guys." Both dogs gave him looks—Diego's pleading, Diesel's rebellious—and Peter got to hear Caleb's growling voice again. "Inside," he ordered, and both dogs went. "They're outside all day," Caleb said, and Peter realized that the man was justifying himself, maybe even feeling a little guilty. "It won't kill them to spend an evening alone."

"They seem like really lucky dogs," Peter said easily. "Right up to the point where random visitors step on them, I think they've got great lives."

Caleb twisted the lock on the inside of the handle and pulled the door shut behind himself. He looked a little awkward, now that the distraction of the dogs was gone, and Peter gave himself a moment to savor the adorableness of it before gesturing toward the driveway. "You good to go?"

"Yeah, okay." Caleb followed Peter down the steps. "You want me to drive?"

"Doesn't matter. You know where you're going, but I take direction well. Whichever."

"You drive, then." Caleb gave Peter a look that seemed almost like a dare. "People around here might recognize my truck and look to see who's inside."

"And you don't want to be seen with an asshole like me." Great. Peter could laugh it off, but Caleb's attitude didn't bode well for the evening.

Caleb seemed to realize that, as well. "Sorry. That was kinda... we're supposed to be leaving the quarry stuff behind, right?"

"If we can."

"Yeah, if we can." Caleb nodded. "And we're going to have a much better chance of that if I relax a little." He opened the passenger door of Peter's car and ducked inside, and Peter followed on his own side.

They drove in relative silence for a while, apart from Caleb's occasional directions. Peter tried to restrain his urge to jump in with small talk. He could be charming if he needed to be; he knew that. He could draw Caleb out, make him feel special and admired, and it wouldn't be a lie, because Caleb *was* special, and Peter *did* admire him. It wouldn't be a lie, but Peter was pretty sure it would *feel* like a lie to Caleb. So he tried to be quiet, tried to restrain his natural impulses as long as he could, and just as he was about to break, Caleb finally spoke.

"So... where did you grow up? In a city?"

"Montreal," Peter confirmed. "Outremont." He wanted to say more, but didn't want to get carried away. "I love it there, but I like Toronto too. How about you? Have you always lived in Rocky Creek?" Peter tried to forget the information he'd already gathered about Caleb's early life. He'd heard all he needed to for business, but this was now personal, and Peter wanted to hear Caleb's version of his life.

"In or around, yeah. I mean, I've spent a few months at a time other places, for jobs. But Rocky Creek's always been my home. Not always on the farm... apartments, usually, or other rentals. My mom moved us a lot. But she never took us too far from here."

Peter could almost feel the effort it was taking for Caleb to avoid a comment about not wanting to see the place ruined with a damned quarry. He decided to remove the temptation. "I like the peace and quiet, and the lack of traffic, but I miss restaurants. And shopping. Dry cleaners."

Caleb looked down at himself, and the self-consciousness was almost painful. "I only have one suit... for weddings and funerals, mostly. Nothing else needs dry cleaning. And I don't do a lot of shopping."

"Maybe that's because you *can't*." But it wasn't something Peter wanted to dwell on. "You look pretty damn good in jeans and a work shirt, anyway. And you're cleaned up real pretty tonight." He wished there were more light in the car so he could see if Caleb was blushing.

"I'm probably underdressed," Caleb said, and he sounded like he was taking it pretty seriously. "I don't go to the city all that often. Not for dinner, at least."

"You look good." Peter didn't dress up the truth, just left it there for Caleb to absorb. When he figured it had been long enough, he asked, "So where do you meet people, then? Guys, I mean. I guess I should have checked earlier, but you're not seeing anyone right now?"

"No." Caleb snorted. "I joke about that, sometimes. That I caused myself a lot of unnecessary pain when I came out, because it's not like there's anyone around to actually be gay *with*." A pause, then, "God, I must sound like a total loser."

"No." Again, Peter didn't need to lie. "You sound like someone who wanted to be honest with people, and wanted them to accept him for who he is. And you sound like someone who loves his land enough to stand by it, even if it's not always convenient."

"Inconvenient? Is that what a total lack of a love life is?"

"Wait a second... we're not talking... like, a *total* lack of a love life? I mean, ever?" Peter wished he wasn't driving, because he'd really like to be able to stare at Caleb until he answered.

But Caleb shook his head with a little laugh. "No, I'm not quite *that* badly off." Then he paused. "Well... 'love'... I guess never on that. But I've, you know... like I said, I've been other places. And there *are* gay guys down here; they just don't advertise. Kinda ironic, I guess... before I came out, I could hook up with them because we were all on the down-low, but once I was out they didn't want to be seen with me. And most of them moved away pretty quick, once they could." He twisted in his seat so he could look at Peter more directly. "How does it work, for you? I mean, in the city, how do you meet people?"

"Friends of friends, coworkers, parties, the occasional bar hookup... lots of ways, really." Peter had never thought too much about it. "I met my last serious relationship at a friend's Super Bowl party."

"Your *last* serious relationship. How many have there been?" Caleb sounded taken aback.

"Not that many. Three, I guess. Well, four. I mean... I didn't really figure it all out until college. So a couple girlfriends before that, but nothing serious, for obvious reasons. Then the obligatory older man, when I was at university. That was more serious for me than for him, but it lasted, off and on, for about three years. Broke up with him for a guy in my MBA program, broke up with *him* when he got kind of weirdly possessive and stalkerish. Then a guy I met at the gym... again, off and on for a year or so. Then Marty, the Super Bowl guy. We were pretty serious, I guess. He moved in, actually, but it was one of those 'his lease was up and he needed somewhere to stay and it just sort of expanded without me noticing' things. We broke up about four months ago."

Caleb was silent for a while, then said, "And there have been guys in between too, right? Like, casual stuff, between the relationships."

"Yeah." Peter had never thought about it. He'd never been tempted to come up with a list of his encounters, but in the face of Caleb's reaction, he was starting to think about numbers. "I'm always careful. Condoms, and all."

"Of course, yeah. I didn't think... I wasn't thinking you were dirty, or something. It's just... wow. You have a *lot* more experience than I do. A *lot*."

"Is that bad?" Peter wasn't sure where this conversation was going, but he didn't think he liked it. "It's circumstances, mostly, right? I mean, I'm not out on the prowl every night or anything. I just... the opportunities presented themselves." That didn't sound quite right. "Not that I'm sleeping with every guy I see! Just... you know. Sometimes I meet someone I like, and he likes me back, and it works out."

"You're interested, you're attracted, you pursue." Caleb's voice was tight as it repeated Peter's words from days earlier.

"Sometimes, yeah." Peter wondered if he should pull over so they could have a better conversation about this. It was really hard to read Caleb's expressions with the occasional glances permitted by driving on an unfamiliar road after dark. "Are you okay? Is this a problem? I mean, you didn't think I was a virgin or something, did you?"

Caleb shook his head slowly. "No, I didn't think that." He paused, and when he spoke again, it felt like he'd made a decision. "And it's not a problem. Of course. Everything's fine."

Peter was tempted to push a little further on that, but he resisted the urge. Whatever Caleb was worried about, the guy didn't seem inclined to share, so Peter would try to respect that, at least for a while.

He followed Caleb's directions to a cozy Mexican restaurant, and they made small talk through the meal. They had common taste in books and movies, but dramatically different preferences in music, and it was fun to argue over something so inconsequential. Caleb's appreciation of both Metallica and Garth Brooks, while completely incomprehensible, was not a serious threat to Peter's professional success. And Peter's insistence that dance remixes were a valid form of artistic expression wasn't going to ruin Caleb's ancestral home.

When they weren't talking, Peter enjoyed just looking. Caleb's face wasn't delicate, exactly; his skin was fairly dark, and he had a scar through one eyebrow and another along his jawline; faint, but enough to roughen him up a little. Peter considered asking about the scars, but he remembered what Riva had said about Caleb being gay-bashed after coming out, and he didn't want to bring up a painful memory. He'd rather spend his energy trying to think about how he'd describe Caleb, if he had to. Not delicate. Not fragile. Fine-boned? Sure, that worked, but it didn't capture the expressiveness of Caleb's eyes, the lushness of his lips, the fine trace of stubble that Peter wanted to feel against his own cheeks, under his own lips. What was it about Caleb that was so attractive? It seemed almost mystical, as if Caleb's connection to his farm had made him some sort of—

"You okay over there?" The check had come and been split, at Caleb's insistence, and they were sipping coffee and relaxing. Apparently, Peter had relaxed to the point that he was no longer being social and Caleb had to check in on him.

"Sorry, yeah." Peter smiled. "Have you ever wondered what your spirit animal would be? I mean, if they existed? I was trying to figure it out, sort of." It wasn't exactly what Peter had been thinking, but it was as close as he could come in words.

"You were trying to figure out my spirit animal? Seriously?"

"Yeah. I'm thinking maybe a panther. Solitary, and beautiful... likes trees... maybe a mountain lion, to catch your coloring."

"That's how you figure out spirit animals? By matching colors?"

"How do *you* do it?"

"I don't do it. Spirit animals? What does that even mean?" Caleb sounded amused, and Peter liked it. He didn't mind making himself sound like a preteen girl, not if it made Caleb happy.

"I don't know. Just a match, I guess. I think I'm going to stick with mountain lion. I wonder if they're really territorial."

Caleb raised an eyebrow. "So what's *your* animal? The army

ant? Moving in a seemingly inevitable wave, consuming and destroying every living thing in its path?"

Ouch. Maybe Peter shouldn't have said that about being territorial. But Caleb was frowning apologetically. "Sorry. That was an overreaction."

Peter shrugged. "Don't worry about it." And then, to get the evening back to the right tone, he raised his head proudly and said, "I've always thought I shared an affinity with the mighty lion."

"You've got a nice mane; I'll give you that." Caleb squinted at Peter. "But I'm going to go with a horse. A palomino, if coloring is so important to you, but something more social than a lion. Or maybe a bird, in a big flock. Or a tropical fish." He grinned. "A shark, in a feeding frenzy. But that would blow your 'must be the same color' rule."

"Damn, I am a lot of animals."

"Or maybe I just don't know you well enough yet. Maybe your true spirit animal can only be discovered by those who know you best."

"For someone who doesn't even know what spirit animals are, you have got some interesting ideas about them. I'm sticking with lion."

"I've heard it's the lionesses that do all the work. And I've got to say, Riva always seems pretty busy...."

Peter really wanted to kiss him. He wanted to kiss him until his smirk faded into stillness, and then gasps. Damn it. That idea about being friends until the timing was right was good in theory, but it sucked in practice. It was hard to be friends with someone you wanted more from, and Peter wanted a *hell* of a lot more from Caleb. "You want to get out of here?" he asked, and realized he should have waited a little longer, until he had his voice under better control. As it was, the simple words came out with a trace of desperation, a hoarseness that made the suggestion into an indecent proposal.

Caleb's eyes widened, but he nodded. The smirk was gone, replaced by a serious intensity that Peter was pretty sure was mirrored on his own face. This was going way faster than he'd planned, but he'd be damned if he'd be the one to stop it.

They made it out of the restaurant, but that was about the limit of Peter's self-control. One brush from Caleb's fingers against Peter's hand, a touch so light that it could have been accidental, and Peter went for it. He spun, brought Caleb with him, pinned the smaller man against the brick wall they were walking beside and leaned in. One hand was on Caleb's belt buckle, although Peter couldn't remember having put it there, and the other held one of Caleb's hands up over his head. It felt predatory, too aggressive, but when Peter leaned in, Caleb surged forward to meet him, their mouths joining with a hungry moan. Peter couldn't have said which of them had made the sound.

The kiss was nothing like their earlier, chaste exchange. This was deep and powerful, lips and tongues and teeth, challenging and encouraging each other, and it was a damn good thing there was a wall to brace against or they might have fallen right over. Peter kept one hand locked onto Caleb's, above their heads, but his other roamed across Caleb's hard abs, up over his chest, behind his neck to pull him forward, down his free arm, tight against his ass, and then, finally, back to its original home on Caleb's belt.

Peter let his fingers spread out a little, eased them beneath the fabric of Caleb's waistband, and then there were voices. A happy, laughing group leaving the restaurant, and Peter remembered where they were. He and Caleb jerked away from each other simultaneously. Peter stood still and took a deep breath, but Caleb turned on his heel and started walking, fast and purposeful, toward the car. It wasn't clear whether he was escaping from the scenario or just heading for a more appropriate venue, but it didn't really matter. Peter followed him. The way he was feeling right then, Peter would have followed Caleb anywhere.

Chapter Seventeen

Caleb needed to calm down. But, God, he also needed to touch Peter, to be touched in return, to find somewhere quiet and private where he could explore the rangy body that had pressed him against the wall with such confidence and power. He tried to breathe more slowly, and he kept walking even after he got to the car.

"Caleb?" he heard from behind him, and he raised an arm in response.

"I just need a minute," he said. He hoped that was true. The movement helped, and the cool night air, but he wasn't sure it would be enough, not if he got another look at Peter, and certainly not if Peter touched him.

He stopped walking at the edge of the parking lot, and Peter's feet crunched through the loose gravel behind him. "You okay?" Peter asked.

"Yeah. Sorry. But that was not being friends. That was not the plan." Caleb kept himself turned away, and Peter seemed to know enough not to come any closer.

"No. It wasn't the plan for me, either. The 'friends' thing is maybe not going to work super well."

It felt good to laugh, even just the little snort that Caleb managed to drive from his tight chest. "You think?"

"But I don't want to walk away, Caleb. I don't know what we can do, but I'd really hate to lose this entirely."

What did that even mean? Caleb wanted to ask. What was the *this* that might be lost? Was Peter thinking of them as a potential relationship, or was Caleb just another one of his casual tricks? A relationship didn't make sense... it wasn't just geography that would get between them; it was their whole lives, their mindsets, their everything. No. Whatever this was, it wasn't anything serious. It couldn't be. And Caleb had too much going on in his life to be this emotionally invested in something that was doomed to fail.

"I think we should go home," Caleb said. "That was a mistake. It was a moment of weakness, or something. You're right, friends isn't going to work, and it doesn't make sense to try for anything else."

Peter was silent for longer than Caleb expected, but finally he said, "Yeah. Okay." A shuffled step in the gravel, and then, "So, you're okay? You're coming back to the car?"

A forty-five minute drive, locked in a confined space with the man who had just made Caleb's blood run hotter than it ever had before. *Okay* wasn't anything like the right word. "Yeah. I'm coming back." Because there was no other way home. And because as stupid as it was, Caleb wanted just a little more time with Peter.

So he went to the car, got into the passenger seat, and tried to relax as Peter guided them out into traffic and headed for home. It had been a good dinner. Fun. Easy. Sure, there had been an undercurrent of attraction, but it had stayed where it belonged, below the surface. Caleb just had to get back to feeling like that. The flare-up outside the restaurant, *that* had been the anomaly. The typical interaction was the casual teasing and friendliness. Right. That would work.

"Maybe a penguin," he tried.

Peter looked at him as if doubting his sanity. "Maybe a penguin what?"

"Your spirit animal. Maybe it's a penguin. They're very social.

How do you feel about eating fish? Being cold? Getting dressed up?"

"They aren't actually wearing tuxes, you know." Peter sounded like he was making an effort, at least. "That's their fur."

"Feathers."

"No, I think it's fur."

"How could it possibly be fur? They're birds." Caleb dared to look over for the reaction.

"Barely." Peter's lips twitched. "I think they're the only egg-laying mammal."

"That's the platypus. And, now that I think about it, maybe the *platypus* is your spirit animal. They're completely weird, and they know very little about penguins, so I'd say you're a pretty good match."

Peter smiled, but didn't respond, and they drove in silence for a while. Caleb leaned his head back against the headrest and closed his eyes. He listened to the thrum of the engine, sensed the car responding easily to Peter's guidance, and felt perfectly safe. God, if he could have this. This sensation of safety, combined with the passion he'd been tantalized by outside the restaurant. If he were offered those two things, with this man... what wouldn't he give up to have them? He wasn't seriously considering it, because he knew it wasn't on the table, not long-term, but what if it were? What would Caleb say if Peter asked him to sell the farm, move to the city, and be with him like this forever?

Caleb knew what he'd say. He'd say he couldn't give up the only security he'd ever known, the only home he'd ever wanted, for a crazy, unlikely chance at love. He couldn't do it, couldn't risk it. But it was fun to dream about.

And, he realized with a start, dreaming was exactly what he'd been doing. He'd drifted off, fallen asleep in the comfortable seat of Peter's sedan, and he was wakened not by the slowing of the car, but by Peter's muttered, "What the fuck?" from the seat beside him.

Caleb sat up and looked around. They were at the bottom of his driveway, just turning in, and Peter was staring up the drive, staring at the house.

It took Caleb a moment to realize this wasn't part of his dream, part of a nightmare. "Oh my God," he said, and Peter stepped on the gas to go more quickly up the drive.

The house was in flames. The stone-walled front of the house was billowing smoke through the roof, and fire danced behind the narrow windows. The back of the house, although it should have been more flammable since it was made of wood, didn't seem to be quite as far gone. But even as Peter jerked the car to a stop, Caleb saw that the back windows were glowing in a way they never should, and he knew the flames had spread back there as well.

Peter had his phone out, and they both opened their doors and got out, staring at the flames as Peter spoke to the emergency operator. Caleb started walking toward the house, and then he broke into a jog. He was almost to the back porch when he felt a strong arm wrap around him from behind and pull him away. "Caleb, it's too late!" Peter yelled over the roaring flames. "You can't do anything now. Wait for the fire trucks."

But Peter didn't understand. "The dogs," Caleb said, and he saw the realization hit Peter's face. "They're inside. I locked them inside. I need to try to get them out." He twisted free and ran for the back door. He had enough presence of mind to pull his sleeve down over his hand before he turned the knob. It was locked, of course, and he fumbled for his key. Where the hell was it? He was losing precious seconds; the fire was growing and the dogs were stuck in there, and he'd been the one to lock them inside. And then he was shoved to the side and Peter was there, smashing a rock through the side window and reaching inside, his own hand covered by his sleeve, to unlock the door.

Hot air blasted out through the broken window and then the open door, and the sound of burning and destruction was almost deafening. The air was thick, palpably full of smoke and embers and loss. Caleb remembered to crouch down to get beneath the worst of it, and then moved forward as quickly as he could. "Diego!" he yelled. "Diesel!" Where would they go? Where would they feel safest; where would they seek comfort?

"Not upstairs," Peter yelled when Caleb looked toward the stairway. "It's too dangerous, Caleb. If they're up there, it's too late."

It was too late already, Caleb was afraid. The dogs hadn't heard the broken glass, hadn't heard his calls. But he had to keep trying, had to keep going. He pushed forward into the kitchen. The smoke was so thick there Caleb could barely see, and he felt Peter grabbing hold of his belt, not to restrain him, but to be guided. Peter was following Caleb into this hell, willingly, and Caleb knew he should feel guilty, but he just felt grateful.

And then he saw them. Lying down, together, and that was something, at least, if this was the end. It was something that they'd met it together. But he rushed forward to where the dogs were sprawled under the table, because maybe it wasn't the end at all. He grabbed the closest one by the ruff and dragged him along toward the door. He was dimly aware of Peter doing the same behind him, and then it was all just the struggle. He was fighting for breath, trying desperately to find any oxygen that hadn't been consumed by the fire, and embers were falling on him, smoking through his clothes and into his skin. The dog was heavy, and the angle was awkward, and how much farther could he possibly go without a proper breath of air?

He felt the first rush of cool air like a benediction. He knew it was bringing more oxygen to fuel the fire that was destroying his home, but it meant he was almost outside, almost out of hell. It gave him the strength to keep going, still dragging the dog along with him, and then he was through the doorway, gasping and retching. He fought onward, stumbling and crawling until the grass beneath him changed from scorched to dew-damp. He looked back and saw Peter behind him.

The man's face was streaked with soot and tears and he was still choking, yet he looked at Caleb and managed a smile as he held out his bleeding hand. "The fucker bit me," he said, and he looked down at the dog he was dragging. "So I bet I've got Diesel."

"Is he still breathing?" Caleb was almost afraid to find out, but he ran his hand over Diego's ribs and felt them move.

"Yeah, he is," Peter reported. He looked around. "The fire trucks will have oxygen, I think. But I don't know how long it will take for them to get here."

"Too long," Caleb decided. "It's a volunteer department, and a long drive. The vet's just on the edge of town, and he lives next door to the clinic. You drive; I'll call and get him ready."

Peter stood, staggered, and then bent and gathered Diesel in his arms. The dog struggled a little, and growled, and it was the sweetest sound Caleb had heard in a long time. "It's okay, Diesel," he said. "He's a friend."

CHAPTER EIGHTEEN

IT FELT natural to stand there behind Caleb, one arm wrapped around his chest for support, as the vet explained the animals' injuries. Some burns, some cuts, probably from broken glass, but most seriously, smoke inhalation.

"It's great that they've made it this far, but there's been some pretty serious damage to their respiratory systems," the doctor said. "We're going to keep them lightly sedated, and monitor them in case the swelling gets to the point that they need to be intubated. We'll give them oxygen and fluids and antibiotics and keep them comfortable so they can heal." The vet absentmindedly ruffled his fingers through the fur on Diego's shoulder, and the gesture made Peter like the man even more than he already did. "We're going to do all we can, but you need to understand that they're still at serious risk for the next several days. And you need to understand that it'll be fairly expensive." He smiled sadly. "Caleb, I've known you since you were a boy. If I didn't think there was a good chance of a full recovery or if I thought their suffering was going to be unmanageable, I'd recommend that you put them down. I do think there's a good chance of recovery. But as I said, it'll be expensive."

Caleb straightened a little, and for the first time since the fire, Peter felt like his support wasn't really needed. "Like you said, Dr. Rivkin, you've known me since I was a boy. I'll pay the bills."

"I didn't mean it like that, Caleb. I know you'll be responsible about it. I just wanted to be sure you understood what you're getting into."

"Make them better," Caleb said simply.

The vet nodded. "Okay. Good." He stepped back and swung the cage door shut to enclose Diego. "We're going to keep them out of it tonight, so there's no reason for you to be here. They won't know or care. Tomorrow we'll lighten the sedation, and if you want to come by, I'm sure they'd like to see you. Depending on how things go, we may keep Diesel sedated a bit longer, since he's not exactly tractable—especially in a frightening situation."

"Or I can be here. If it's better for him not to be sedated, I can be here. He'll do as he's told if I'm here."

"Okay. Give me a call tomorrow, and we'll see where we are on that." The doctor glanced at Peter, then back at Caleb. "Do you have somewhere to stay? I'm truly sorry about the house, Caleb."

Peter felt Caleb tense. Worrying about the dogs had distracted Caleb from thinking about the house, but the reality had to hit him sooner or later. "You can stay with me, if you want," Peter offered, then hastened to add, "There's two beds. Or I can try to get you another room at the motel, but I think they're pretty much full, between us and Penny."

"I don't want to be a nuisance," Caleb said. "I could call Matt and stay in their guest room. It's just...." he faded out, then he said, "I don't want to disturb them, either."

"I'm sure they'd be happy to have you, Caleb, but so would I, and I'm already awake." Peter looked at his watch. "I know you're tired, but the cops wanted to talk to you, and they said they wanted to talk to me, too, since I'm a bit of a witness." Caleb seemed undecided, almost dazed, and Peter didn't want to be pushy, but he didn't think Caleb was really up to making any decisions. "So why don't I tell them to meet us at the motel. We can shower, I can lend you some clothes, and we've got an office set up, so you can talk to the police in there. Is that okay?"

"I don't want to be a nuisance," Caleb repeated, but Peter could tell he wasn't really objecting.

"You're not the nuisance, the cops are. I have to stay up and talk to them anyway, so I may as well stay up with you. Okay?"

"Yeah, okay," Caleb agreed. He stuck his fingers through the bars of each dog's cage, reaching far enough in to reach Diego's ear and one of Diesel's paws, then turned resolutely and headed for the door.

Peter stayed behind for just a moment. "If something happens... something bad," he said, and he knew the vet understood what he meant, "call me, okay?" He reached into his jacket pocket and pulled out a card. "The cell number. The dogs are all he has left. If something bad happens, I want to be there for him."

The vet took the card and nodded. "The dogs *are* very important to him," he agreed. "But from the sound of things, they're not quite *all* he has left." His smile was gentle, and it stayed in Peter's mind as he followed Caleb out the door and over to the sedan.

He carefully drove the few blocks to the motel, then got out and waited for Caleb. It took longer than it should have. "Caleb?" he said gently. "Caleb, man, should we be going to the doctor? We both got a good dose of the crap from the house, and my lungs are feeling pretty scorched. We've both been coughing for hours. And you're kind of out of it. Do you want to go to the doctor?"

Caleb stared at the pavement, then looked up at Peter. "I want to go home," he said simply. It didn't sound like he was deranged, thankfully. It didn't sound like he thought he actually *could* go home. Instead, it was a heartbreaking acknowledgement that he couldn't.

"Fuck, Caleb, I know. I'm really, really sorry."

"It makes it easier for you. Doesn't it? Without the house, why would I fight? Without the house, I'll just give up, right? And you'll have one less voice yelling about the quarry."

"Bullshit," Peter said. He was pretty sure Caleb wasn't accusing him of anything, but he didn't like the attitude anyway. "You'll still fight. I'm sorry your house is gone, I truly am. But you'll keep fighting. You'll fight for the farmland. The topsoil, and the way it's fed this community for generations. You'll fight for the fucking winter wheat, Caleb. Those little shoots, hibernating under the snow, waiting for the springtime so they can grow." Caleb's brown eyes were deep and sad, but they were watching Peter intently, and Peter smiled. "You'll keep fighting, Caleb."

"I'm tired."

Peter was pretty sure Caleb meant something more than just being sleepy, but he let himself focus on the easy fix. "So come inside, have a shower, and you can have a nap while I sort things out with the cops. If we're lucky, they'll wait until tomorrow to talk to us." He stepped up beside Caleb, nudged him toward the door, unlocked it, and guided Caleb inside.

"Bathroom's over there," he indicated, not that there was much room for doubt. "You can have first shower."

Caleb nodded, but didn't move his feet. Fuck. Was this some sort of oxygen-loss thing, or just the shock of having lost his home? The former seemed unlikely. Caleb had been efficient and alert on the way to the vet and the entire time the dogs were being worked on. And Peter had inhaled pretty much the same stuff Caleb had, and he felt... well, he felt gross, but not mentally impaired. "Caleb... look, man, you can just sleep if you want to, with no shower, but I really think you'll feel better if you get cleaned up. I can't smell us anymore, but I bet we reek of smoke. Probably some crazy-ass chemicals too."

Caleb nodded and began absentmindedly unbuttoning his shirt. Well, Peter hadn't exactly expected the undressing to start right there, but he certainly didn't mind. But Caleb stopped with only a few buttons undone and turned to look at Peter. "What do you think started it?" he asked.

"I have no idea." Anything he could think of would sound like he was accusing Caleb of being careless. Not a good idea right then, he figured. "They'll have a fire investigator, I imagine. Your insurance company will want one, even if the cops don't." And then a nasty thought. "You *were* insured, right?"

Caleb nodded. "Yeah."

"Okay." Peter wasn't sure if it was a good idea, but he eased over to stand in front of Caleb and lifted his hands to the front of Caleb's soot-stained shirt. "I can help you, if you want," he said, and he slowly undid one of the buttons. Caleb moved, and Peter jerked his hands back, but then he realized that Caleb had been dropping his arms, giving in to Peter's ministrations.

"Does china burn?" Caleb asked as Peter eased the shirt off his shoulders. "My grandmother's china was in there. I never used it. Didn't really like the pattern. But it was hers. Do you think it burned?"

"Arms up," Peter instructed, and he slid Caleb's undershirt up and over his head. "I don't know about china. I mean, I don't think it would burn. But it might have gotten broken. I don't know."

Caleb nodded, and Peter sat on the bed and bent down to reach Caleb's shoes. "Left foot," he instructed, and Caleb obediently lifted that foot and let Peter slide off his shoe and sock. "Right foot," Peter said, and they repeated the process.

"The fireplace," Caleb said. "It's... it's made to stand up to fire. It couldn't burn."

"I guess not," Peter agreed. It wasn't like Caleb was really looking for expertise. He unbuckled Caleb's belt, trying to forget how the leather had felt beneath his fevered hands just a few short hours earlier, and then found the button and zipper of Caleb's fly. He shoved the fabric back and down over Caleb's hips, and that was as far as he was going to go. If Caleb couldn't get his boxer briefs off by himself, he could just shower in them. A man had to know his limits. "Okay, then, come on." He headed for the bathroom, and Caleb followed him. "The towels are on the hook here. There's shower gel in there, and shampoo." Peter reached into the shower and turned the water on. When he tested it a moment later, it felt scalding on the spots of his hand that had been burned by embers, and he turned the temperature down. "It's a little cool, so don't stay in there for too long."

He turned and put both of his hands on Caleb's shoulders. "Caleb. Stay with me, here. You're going to get all the way undressed, get in the shower, wash yourself and your hair, get out, and put on the sweatpants and T-shirt that I'll leave on the vanity. Okay?" Caleb didn't really respond, and Peter's concern came very close to being alarm. "Caleb? I'm not fucking with you, here. If you can't do this, we're going to find a doctor, okay? I need to see some functioning, now."

After a too long moment, Caleb lifted his eyes and squinted at Peter's face. "A squirrel, maybe. One of those bossy little bastards who sits up on a branch and scolds me when I go out to feed the birds."

Peter's relief made his laugh a little too loud, but he didn't care. "Yeah, okay, that's my spirit animal. A tree-rat. Nice. Get your ass in the shower and get cleaned up." He shook Caleb's shoulders gently, affectionately. "Don't worry, everything will still be all fucked up when you get out."

Caleb's return smile was weak, but at least he was trying. "That's not really all that reassuring."

"I never said I was good at this. Now, get in there." Peter turned and walked purposefully out the door. He'd grab clothes for Caleb, then run next door to the office room and have a quick shower there. Hopefully he'd be back before Caleb got himself dressed and together, and then Peter could put Caleb to bed and find somewhere quiet where he could call the cops. The whole thing was pretty damn complicated, and it wasn't altogether clear just what he was doing in the middle of it. But somehow, it felt like exactly where he was meant to be.

Chapter Nineteen

Caleb woke to the sound of an unfamiliar ringtone. Then there was a rustle of frantic movement, and a hushed, familiar voice saying, "Hang on," presumably into the phone. More movement, a door opening and shutting, and Caleb finally opened his eyes.

They felt dry, the lids stiff, and it took a moment for him to understand where he was, and why he felt so awful. He was distracted from his memories by a violent burst of coughing. He swung his legs over the side of the bed and sat up, but that seemed to just move the crap in his lungs around a little and make him cough even more.

He was gasping for air by the time he finally got himself under control, and it seemed only natural to lean into the strong chest that had somehow arranged itself beside him. Peter lifted a glass of water in front of Caleb's face, and Caleb reached for it gratefully.

"How come you're not coughing?" he asked after taking a careful sip.

"I was up for a few hours last night, hacking up a lung in the next room. I guess I got it out of my system then." Peter's voice *was* a little more gravelly than usual.

"Thank you," Caleb said, and he took another sip.

"No worries. I can get you something to eat too, if you want."

"I don't mean for the water. Well, yeah, thanks for the water.

But I mean... everything. The bed, and getting me cleaned up, and... the dogs. You could have gotten hurt, following me in there. You could have died."

Peter's arm wrapped around Caleb's shoulder and gave him a quick, hard squeeze, but when he spoke, his voice was light. "Nah. Penguins are practically invincible. Highly flame-retardant."

"They really aren't."

"They *act* like they aren't. It's all part of their secret identity."

Caleb smiled softly. "That's what I thought about you, when I first saw you. That night at the town hall meeting."

"You thought I was a penguin, even then?"

"I thought you were a superhero. You seemed so strong and confident. And beautiful." Caleb had no idea why he was talking like this. Maybe because being embarrassed about his crush was less painful than thinking about his house.

Another squeeze, and a gentle kiss to Caleb's temple. They sat in comfortable silence until another coughing fit hit, and Peter grabbed the glass of water away before Caleb spilled it. When Caleb finally relaxed back into Peter's arms and reclaimed his drink, Peter gave him another kiss, nearer to his ear this time. And it was then that Caleb saw the gauze bandage wrapped tidily around Peter's hand.

"He bit you," Caleb said, remembering. "Diesel... he bit you! Oh, shit, Peter, you know he didn't mean it, right? And he's had all his shots and everything. But still...."

"Not such a superhero now, am I? Got bitten by an almost unconscious dog." He let Caleb take his hand, but there was really nothing to see but bandage. "It's fine, Caleb." Peter sounded like he was smiling, but Caleb couldn't bring himself to look and be sure. "He broke the skin, but he was nowhere near full strength. I checked with the vet last night, and he said the same thing you did about Diesel having his shots. And I got a tetanus shot just a couple months ago, so I'm fine. It's not a big deal."

"My dog bit you as you were risking your life trying to save his. How is that not a big deal?"

"'Cause it's not. 'Cause I'm fine." Caleb finally looked at Peter, and he was rewarded with a fond, gentle smile. Peter's face grew more serious as he said, "But the cops called this morning." He scoffed at Caleb's expression. "Not about the dog, you psycho! How could they know about that?" Caleb felt like there was maybe another quick kiss coming, but he was disappointed. Instead, Peter got serious again. "They want to come by."

Caleb nodded. He supposed he couldn't hide from the truth forever. His home, the house that had been passed down to him through generations, was gone. There were procedures to be followed, and then Caleb would have to try to find a way to deal with the hole left in his life.

But Peter seemed to think there was more to be said. "Caleb... they're treating it as a crime scene. Suspected arson. They've got a team of investigators coming down."

"A crime scene? They think somebody set the fire?" Caleb straightened up and turned to stare at Peter. "They think *I* set the fire?"

"I don't think they've gotten that far. And anybody who knows you knows that's crazy. They just said they were treating it as suspicious. I don't know, man, maybe they treat *all* fires as suspicious."

Caleb's thoughts were fragmented, scattered. He tried to focus on the things he could control. "The barn... it's a long way from the house. It's fine, right?"

Peter shrugged. "I don't know. They didn't mention it."

"The animals were mostly out in the pasture—the horses and the cattle and the goat. The chickens roost in the barn, but there's a door for them to get out. Those guys should be fine. But they need to be checked on. Am I... is it a crime scene, like, I'm not allowed to go there? Somebody needs to check on the animals."

"Let's get the cops over here, okay? They'll have answers to all that stuff. I don't think they're investigating you personally, but if you're uncomfortable with their questions, we'll stop the interview and get a lawyer, okay?"

"Aren't *you* a lawyer?" It would be really nice to have someone he trusted in his corner.

"Not criminal law. I mean, I'm a member of the bar, but I don't do this stuff. If it comes down to it, we'll want an expert. But I can be there, if you want."

It occurred to Caleb, finally, just how much he was asking from this man who was barely more than a stranger. It was frightening how easy it was to depend on Peter, but easy didn't mean right. "You have your own stuff to do... I'm sorry. The quarry, and everything...." And then Caleb remembered. "Oh, fuck!"

Peter looked startled. "What?"

"Damn it. Jayne Blythe. She's coming down today, wants to see my shop before I give her lunch. I mean, at least I've got a good excuse for a crappy lunch, other than just not being much of a cook. But is she even going to be allowed on the property?"

Peter's expression was hard to read. "Jayne Blythe? She's... is this normal? She comes down and has a look at your stuff and has lunch?"

This was getting a bit awkward. "No. It's not normal. I called her, after... you know. After your meeting, where you talked her out of supporting us. I called her, and asked if she'd come down. I wanted her to see what was at stake."

Peter nodded. "Yeah. Okay, that's... that's a good move. She'd be valuable." He stood up and forced a smile onto his face. "Right.

I'm not quite sure how to manage this, but you shouldn't tell me any more about that, okay? I mean, I'm bound to do the best job I can for my employers. That's... that's my responsibility. I don't know what I'm supposed to do, if I get information from you that I should be acting on as part of my job."

So there it was. The obstacle that had sent Caleb across the parking lot the night before, back in play. "Yeah." He stood up too, and tried to look energetic and purposeful. "Right." He looked down at himself, wrapped up in Peter's oversized clothes. "I guess I need to borrow these, if that's okay. Just until I can get to the store. And then, if there's no extra room here, I'll call Matt. I should call him anyway, I guess. But I can stay there...."

"I'm not kicking you out, Caleb. You're welcome to stay here. And I'm happy to help. The quarry stuff isn't going anywhere—this is more important. I'm just saying that you shouldn't give me details, okay? That's all."

"Doesn't it look bad for you? Won't your boss think you're... you know, sleeping with the enemy?"

"If my boss actually thought I was sleeping with the enemy, she'd probably give me a raise. They're pretty out-of-the-box thinkers. But you're not the enemy, Caleb. You're a valuable participant in the process. And you're a member of the community that I'm supposed to be winning over, so... I'm covered. No worries." Then Peter frowned. "But I guess it's not the same for you. You didn't even want to be seen in the same car as me last night. This probably looks a lot worse."

It made Caleb a bit dizzy to shake his head, but he did it anyway. "No. I don't care what it looks like. They can think what they want to about me."

"You're sure? I get to go home after all this is over, Caleb. You're stuck here. In a good way, I mean. Not stuck, just... these people are your neighbors, for a long time."

And there was no point in throwing that away for some

short-term nothing with a handsome stranger. Caleb got the point, and he supposed it was a sign of Peter's good intentions that he'd bothered to make it. "Like you said, though: I want to be honest with people, and I want them to accept me for who I am." He grinned quickly. "Of course, in this case, they're going to get totally the wrong idea, and probably won't accept me at all. But, whatever. I'm not going to hide."

Peter nodded slowly, as if there was maybe something in there that he wanted to argue with but had decided to leave alone. "Okay. Why don't you call the vet for an update while I call the cops and arrange for them to come by? We've got coffee and cereal and milk in the office, so unless you want a feast, we can have breakfast here. We can ask the cops about the animals, and you can... you can do what you need to do in terms of... anything else that might be happening today. Anyone who might be coming by. If you needed to meet with any over-the-top lobbyists working as PR consultants, I think there's one two doors down. Room 6. Just in case you were interested." Peter raised his eyebrows inquiringly. "You also, of course, have the option of telling me to back off and stop trying to organize you. I can't do much about the cops, but for the rest of them... if you want to just crawl back into bed, I can fend them off and give you some time to recover."

Caleb thought crawling back into bed sounded like a great plan, but he didn't think it would be nearly as much fun if Peter was off dealing with callers. Besides, "So even if you're not *organizing* me, you're still going to be busy *protecting* me. I appreciate it, I do, but it's making me feel like a bit of a leech."

Peter smiled softly. "I guess I kinda liked the 'superhero' thing. So you'd be helping me out, here. If I'm thinking about a job change, moving into Super Protective Services, I should try to get some on-the-job experience before I do anything drastic."

Caleb knew he should argue more, but he also knew he wasn't going to. "Thank you," he said, and he was rewarded with a smile.

"You're welcome. Now, I've got a phone call to make, and possibly you do too. I wouldn't know about that. I'll be next door in the office; you can come over when you want."

Caleb watched Peter as he opened the door between the adjoining rooms and carefully closed it behind himself, leaving Caleb in privacy. Caleb couldn't think about the house. Not yet. So he let himself think about Peter instead. It might all be a silly pipe dream, but it was a fun one, and Caleb figured he deserved a little fantasy.

CHAPTER TWENTY

PETER had never really thought of himself as a nurturer before. He wasn't an asshole, he didn't think, but he'd never had that instinct to look after somebody, to comfort and pamper them. Not until now. He looked down at the bowl of cereal he was holding, and resolutely took a mouthful. Yes, it was his second bowl of the day. Yes, when he'd poured it, he'd been thinking of sneaking in and leaving it next to Caleb, just in case he needed something to eat. Peter took another mouthful. Yes, he was in *way* over his head.

Riva, of course, had noticed his behavior, even if she wasn't clear on the thought process behind it. "You can't use the same bowl twice, now? How much of a princess are you?"

"I am a complete princess," Peter said, and he let a bit of milk and cereal drool out of his mouth and back into the bowl.

"Eww," Riva laughed. "My six-year-old nephew does stuff like that."

"Your six-year-old nephew is on his way to being one hell of a guy. Or else a bit of a princess. Hard to be sure." He thought he heard movement from the other room and turned to stare at the door, but it didn't open.

Of course, Riva noticed *that* too. She didn't say anything at first. She just smirked, and then she walked past him on the way to the photocopier and ruffled his hair as if he were, in fact, her six-year-old nephew. It wasn't until she sat down at her desk that she gave the door a meaningful look of her own and then said, "You know, Peter, lately I've been asking myself a silly little question. Do you want to hear it?"

"No." He stuffed another spoonful of cereal into his mouth.

She smiled beatifically. "You probably don't *need* to hear it, do you? Because you're asking the exact same question yourself."

"No, I'm not," he mumbled through the cereal in his mouth.

"I think you are."

It was good that the door to the other room opened then, because otherwise the conversation would certainly have degenerated even further. And it was good that the door opened because it was Caleb who came through it, and Peter had decided that seeing Caleb was always a good thing.

"Breakfast?" he offered as Caleb looked shyly in Riva's direction.

"Morning, Caleb," Riva said, standing up and walking closer to him. All her playfulness was gone as she said, "I am so sorry about your home. I know how important it was to you. And I'm sorry about the dogs too. Did you call the vet?"

"I did," he said. "They're stable, and Dr. Rivkin said that's the best we could expect. He said an absence of trouble means they're healing."

Peter wanted to go in for the congratulatory hug. He wasn't sure whether it was because he was genuinely *that* relieved about the dogs or just because he wanted to take advantage of any excuse to touch Caleb.

"That's great," Riva said with a warm smile, and then she returned to her work.

"You should eat something," Peter said, more forceful now that his earlier offer had been ignored. "Do you want coffee and cereal, or do you want to walk over to the diner?"

"Coffee and cereal is great, thanks," Caleb said, still a bit shy. It was as if he had to overcome his bashfulness for each new setting he found himself in. Driving in the car, eating in the restaurant, making out in the parking lot, getting undressed in Peter's motel room, sleeping in the bed next to Peter's, resting in Peter's arms between bouts of coughing; these had all been surmounted. But eating cereal in an office was new, and it was making Caleb uncomfortable. It was absolutely charming, but Peter was pretty sure there wasn't much Caleb could do right then that *wouldn't* be charming. Drooling milk and cereal back into his bowl, for example, would be adorable. And it would show Riva whose side Caleb was on, so that would be good too.

"The cops said they'll be by about nine o'clock," Peter said as he headed for the mini-fridge. "After that... you had your wallet with you last night, right? You have credit cards and everything?"

"Yeah, I'm fine for that."

"So maybe you do should some shopping. You can use my toiletries, if you want, but you'd probably rather use the brands you're used to."

"I *saw* your toiletries, Peter. I don't even know what most of that stuff *is*. I need, like, deodorant, a bar of soap, and a razor."

"Heathen." Peter handed a bowl and spoon and the box of cereal to Caleb and carried the milk over to the table. He cleared a spot for Caleb to set down his breakfast and then got them both fresh coffee. He was dimly aware of Riva watching him as he worked, and knew she was laughing at him, but he ignored her. He settled into the chair opposite Caleb and wondered what it would be like for them to have breakfast together in his downtown condo.

For all that Peter had tried to be a gentleman the night before, he'd gotten a pretty good look at the tight, lean muscles of Caleb's chest and stomach, and Peter thought it would be a good idea if Caleb ate future breakfasts shirtless. Or maybe with a shirt on, but undone, soft cotton flowing off his shoulders, open in the middle just enough to give Peter tantalizing glimpses of the skin underneath. A shirt like that, open just right, was practically an engraved invitation for Peter's hand, or his mouth, and Caleb would damn well know it, the tease! Maybe that was their Sunday morning game, each of them tantalizing the other, trying not to be the first to lose control. Yeah, they could do that. But Peter was pretty sure he'd lose, because all Caleb would have to do would be to give him that shy look, like the one he was giving right then....

And then somebody knocked on the door. Peter jumped guiltily to his feet. He hadn't just been mentally undressing the traumatized man across the table from him! He hadn't! He'd been... he'd been doing something else. He wasn't sure just what, and it didn't matter anyway, because he was going to answer the door, and that was more important. Yeah.

He pulled the door open to see two uniformed Ontario Provincial Police officers on the doorstep. "Hey, guys. Come on in." Peter extended his hand. "I'm Peter Carr; this is my associate, Riva Singh; and I think you said you already know Caleb Sinclair?"

"Yeah. Hi, Caleb," the older of the two men said. He shook Peter's hand and said, "I'm Constable Wilson; this is Constable Graham." He turned back to Caleb. "Meggie's still raving about that class she took with you. She wants to know when the next one will be." He stepped forward as Caleb stood up, and said, "No, finish your breakfast. We're sorry to intrude. We just want to get this cleared up as quickly as we can, and let you get back to dealing with the mess." He frowned. "We'll give our report to the insurance agency, with your permission; but your permission is mostly a formality, because they won't pay without it. And they may want their own investigator involved, as well. You've contacted them?"

"Not yet," Caleb admitted.

Wilson frowned. "Okay. Okay, so I'm going to say this once, not because I think I need to, but because I want to be safe.

Okay?"

Caleb looked as surprised as Peter felt, but he nodded cautiously. Wilson said, "If someone was to burn down his own property... that's a minor issue. There'd be a question of permits, or endangering public health, that sort of thing. But it wouldn't be as serious a crime as if he tried to make an insurance claim for the fire." He looked like he didn't really want to continue, but he forged on. "So if someone made a mistake, and did something stupid, but then thought better of it, the best thing for him to do would be to *not* file an insurance claim. That would be a very smart move."

Caleb shook his head firmly. "I didn't burn my house down. I have no idea who did—I don't even know why you guys think it was arson."

"Okay," Wilson said. "That's fine. I just wanted to make the situation clear." He looked around the room. "We'd like to take statements separately, if we could. Is there another room...?"

"Yeah, my bedroom's there," Peter said, gesturing.

Riva stood up. "And I can go into mine, and leave the office for Caleb."

"You don't have to do that," Caleb protested, but Riva just smiled.

"They're identical rooms, Caleb. It doesn't matter where I am." It wasn't quite true; Peter had flipped the beds in the office room up on end to make more room for a few folding tables and desks, but it was a good effort on Riva's part, and he appreciated it.

"Okay, then," Wilson said. "Graham, why don't you take Mr. Carr next door and get set up in there, do the background questions, and I'll come in when I'm done here."

There was something not quite right about that. "Caleb, you remember what I said, right? They're just doing their jobs; it's good to cooperate—but if it starts sounding like they're investigating you for something, you totally have the right to stop the interview and call a lawyer. Okay?"

Caleb nodded. "It's okay, Peter. I don't have anything to hide."

So Peter followed the younger officer into the other room, and he stared at the two unmade beds as the officer set up a video camera, and then Peter sat down where he was told and answered a bunch of questions about where he was from, who he worked for, and what he was doing in town. It was somewhere in the middle of those questions that his concerns started to clarify, and when the older officer walked into the room and closed the door behind him, Peter looked straight at him. "It's taking longer to interview me than to interview Caleb? Why is that? The only connection I have to this is that I was with Caleb when the fire started, and I was with him when he got home."

"We're trying to get a full picture of the situation, Mr. Carr," Wilson said.

"You've *got* a full picture, from Caleb. Why am I being questioned more extensively?"

"We're trying to rule out suspects, Mr. Carr."

"Rule out... rule out suspects, by talking to me? That means you think *I'm* a suspect." It made sense, he realized with a sick feeling. He had motive, or his company did; Caleb's interest in preserving his home was a huge factor in the opposition to the quarry. And Peter had been the one to get Caleb away from the house, ensuring that the crime didn't become murder rather than just arson. "I think a need a lawyer," he said, almost to himself.

Wilson raised his eyebrows. "You saying that... you know, it makes it sound like you have something to hide."

Peter raised his own eyebrows in return. "And you saying that makes it sound like you don't want me to have a lawyer, which makes it crystal clear that I should have one." He stood up. "This interview is over until I have obtained legal counsel. I'll have someone contact you to set up a time for further questions."

Wilson shook his head sadly. "I'm sorry to hear that, Mr. Carr. It's going to be pretty awkward when I have to tell Mr. Sinclair that his new friend is refusing to cooperate with us on this matter."

The weight in Peter's stomach twisted and churned, but he kept his face impassive. "I'm sorry that you'll have to go through that," he said. "Now, if you don't mind, I need to make some calls. You can leave through the office, or through this door. Your call."

"We'll go through the office," Wilson said. "We need to update Mr. Sinclair."

"Fine," Peter managed, and he waited until the officers were out of the room before he sank down onto the bed. He was under investigation for a felony. And Caleb was going to hear all about it. It didn't make sense, but it was the second part that was upsetting him the most.

CHAPTER TWENTY-ONE

"It's ridiculous," Caleb protested. "He was with me the whole time. He didn't even come in the house before we left."

"We're thinking he wasn't acting alone," Wilson said. "We'll be speaking to Ms. Singh before we leave, but there's no reason to believe she was the accomplice. It could have been anyone. But he's the one with the motive."

"No." Caleb shook his head emphatically. He didn't know what else to say. He was tempted to point out the sexism of assuming that Riva couldn't possibly have been the one in charge of such a crime, but he didn't think it would help Peter, and he didn't want to drag Riva into it. So he just shook his head. "No."

"He's the one with the motive," Wilson repeated stubbornly. "I asked you about enemies, and you said none that you knew of. There was the assault, but that was years ago—no reason to think it would flare up now."

"Are you even sure it was arson?" Caleb asked desperately. "Maybe it was faulty wiring, or something. It's an old house."

"We're still gathering evidence, but the preliminary investigation has made it pretty clear." Wilson seemed a bit gentler now. "I'm sorry, Caleb. I'm sure this makes a bad situation even worse." But he was businesslike as he said, "I'll go speak to Ms. Singh now." He held his hand out to Constable Graham. "I'll take the camera, but there's no need for you to come. We don't want her to feel like we're ganging up on her."

They hadn't had the same hesitation with Peter, Caleb reflected, but he didn't object. Getting Constable Graham alone would suit him just fine. So he waited for the older man to leave the room, then turned to the younger officer and said, "It's been a while, Sean. You've been taking care of yourself?"

Graham looked nervously at the door Wilson had just gone through. "I'm at *work*, Caleb."

"You work for the provincial government. They're not going to fire you for being gay."

"Jesus, Caleb, shut up! I don't... not at work, Caleb. No."

"I'm not trying to make trouble, Sean." Caleb didn't know how to feel about what he was planning, but he thought of Peter being suspected of a serious crime, and he knew he was going to do it anyway. "I want to cooperate with you any way I can as you fight to hide your terrible, awful secret." That was maybe laying it on a little thick, but it wasn't like Caleb had practice at this sort of thing. "But I'd appreciate a little cooperation in return. Wilson wouldn't tell me why you guys are so sure it's arson. To me... you know... it's your life, so it's your secret, being gay. That makes sense. But this is *my* life. My house. So why does someone else get to know secrets about it?"

"Jesus, Caleb, I could lose my job."

"And you *couldn't* lose your job for coming out. But you won't do that, and you *will* tell me what I want to know. I have no idea what to make of your priorities."

"What, are you *enjoying* this, now?"

"No." Caleb double-checked. "No. I'm not enjoying it. I'm just trying to find a way for this to make sense. Now, Sean... why are they so sure this is arson? What the hell is going on?"

"Fuck, Caleb." Sean sighed, then said, "The fire started near the hearth, but you said you hadn't had a fire in more than a week. We're testing for chemicals, but the burn pattern makes it clear that an accelerant was used. Probably gasoline, spread all over the floors and walls. Pretty standard."

"Wait." Caleb tried to sort it all out. "The fire was started in the living room? *Inside* the house?" He didn't want to think about it, didn't want to realize what it meant. He didn't want to follow his thoughts where he was afraid they would lead him, not if he was traveling alone. But he didn't have to be alone. And he didn't have to be with Sean Graham, either. He crossed the room in three big strides, opened the door to Peter's room, stepped inside, and closed the door behind him.

Peter was on the bed, cell phone at his ear, but he twisted the mouthpiece away and said, "I had nothing to do with it, Caleb. I swear." He looked like he was ready for Caleb to attack him, and it was bewildering.

"I know that." Caleb stepped closer and squinted down at Peter. "I *know* that," he repeated. "Even before I heard what I just heard, I knew it wasn't you." He sat on the bed by Peter's side, wrapped an arm around his shoulders and then leaned up to press a gentle kiss to his temple. "I know."

Peter nodded slowly and let out a deep breath. "Thank you." He looked at the phone in his hand and then slid the bar to hang up. "I'll call them back," he said. He paused, and then turned the ringer off as well. He set the phone on the bedside table and turned so he could look at Caleb head-on. "What do you mean, before you heard what you just heard? What did you hear?"

Caleb pulled his arm off Peter's shoulders. He looked at the curtain-covered window and tried to think of a way out of what he was thinking. "The fire started in the living room, he said. He said there was accelerant splashed all over the walls, and the floor."

"Okay...."

Caleb sighed. "Someone was in my house, Peter. The fire was started from inside, and it wasn't like they just threw a match through a window, not if they splashed gasoline all over the place."

"That's creepy, I know. Thinking of someone being in there."

Caleb shook his head impatiently. Apparently Peter was going to make him spell it out. "The dogs, Peter. The vet didn't say the dogs had been hurt before the fire started, did he? I don't know if he tested for drugs. I guess probably not. But Diesel won't eat anything from a stranger, so I don't know how anyone could drug him. And there's no way he'd let anyone in the house. Not... not anyone he didn't know." Caleb stopped talking then. He wasn't going to make the final conclusion, not if there was a chance that Peter might do it for him. Or might find a way to help keep him from having to make it.

But Peter was still thinking it through. "The back door was locked," he said. "The windows... were the windows broken? I can't remember, not for sure." And then he said it—not the words Caleb had been waiting for, but the ones that made it clear Peter had reached the same horrible suspicion Caleb had. "Maybe not. Maybe... Maybe the dogs *were* drugged. Or maybe they were just locked out, somehow... there's no door between the front and the back of the house? Maybe it was someone who's just really good with dogs. Or maybe he hit Diesel over the head."

Caleb nodded slowly. Maybe. But he didn't think so. "Or maybe the dogs didn't object to him letting himself in. Maybe they were used to it, because he comes over uninvited all the time. Comes over to mooch dinner from his brother." He looked at Peter, and Peter looked back at him, and then moved, shifted so he could wrap both arms around Caleb's shoulders and pull him in tight. Caleb let himself relax into Peter's strong, comforting body. Getting attached to Peter was signing up for heartache, long-term, and Caleb knew it. But there was too much else going on, too much sapping his strength, and he couldn't resist temptation. He would lean on Peter, for now, and he would hope that by the time the inevitable happened, he'd have regained enough strength to be able to stand on his own.

CHAPTER TWENTY-TWO

PETER wanted to hunt Trevor Sinclair down and beat the shit out of him. He wanted to drag the son of a bitch to the ruins of Caleb's house and grind the bastard's face into the ashes, and he didn't really care if some of the embers were still hot. But he kept a lid on himself, because his emotions were nothing compared to what Caleb must be feeling, and Peter wanted to do anything he could for Caleb.

"It's one possibility. It's something to be looked at. But he's your brother, Caleb. Take it slow, okay? I mean, even in your head, if you can."

"It makes sense, Peter. Think about it. You're the only other person who has a motive, and I know it wasn't you. Not just because I want to trust you. Because you were with me when the fire started, and you risked your life to help me with the dogs. But mostly because you were right: it's not going to make me quit fighting the quarry. And you knew that even before I did, so you knew there was no point to this, not for you." He smiled quickly. "And because this isn't part of the process, is it? We're supposed to be arguing about ideas and facts and theories, not setting shit on fire."

"It's absolutely not part of the process, Caleb." Peter wasn't sure what was going on in his chest, his throat, and for a second he thought maybe the smoke inhalation was coming back to make itself a nuisance again. Then he felt the stinging in his eyes and blinked hard. Jesus, he was not going to *cry*! Not because somebody showed a little basic faith in his character. He took a deep breath, got control of himself, and said, "Okay. Yeah, it does make sense... Trevor wanted to sell; you didn't want to. Now you're more likely to. Or maybe there's insurance money?"

"He's fucking deluded!" Caleb pushed away from Peter and stood up. "The insurance is *in my name.* The deed is *in my name.* There is no way on Earth I'm going to give him any money from that house, not now, not *ever!*"

"*If* you believe he did it." Peter stood up as well; Caleb's energy was infectious, and Peter always liked moving around when he thought. "But maybe he thinks you won't believe it." He caught himself. "Okay, well, maybe he *didn't* do it. That's still a possibility. Maybe it was just some random asshole...."

"Who got into the house past my two huge dogs, one of whom has a serious attitude problem with strangers."

"Yeah, okay, but...." Peter wasn't sure how far he should be pushing this. He wasn't sure if Caleb would be helped more by maintaining a shadow of a doubt or by solving the mystery. "Maybe you should give the vet a call. You could get him to check for drugs, or for signs of a concussion or whatever. If anything like that shows up, this is a whole different conversation."

"And if it doesn't?" Caleb sounded like he was already pretty sure what the vet was going to find.

"If it doesn't, we look at this again. Yeah. We look at *everyone* the dogs would let in... I know, there's probably nobody the dogs like who you don't care about, but...."

"Trevor, Matt, and Sarah. That's it." Caleb's voice was flat.

"No other friends? No... okay, you said you weren't getting a lot of action, but no casual visitors...."

"No. Trevor, Matt, and Sarah. Do you think the doctor and his pregnant wife are arsonists?"

"Mrs. Dean is pregnant? I didn't know that."

"Shit. It's a secret. They've...." Caleb ran his hands through his hair restlessly. "They've had trouble in the past. And she's supposed to be avoiding stress. I wonder if I should call her before she hears it somewhere else."

This whole situation was getting overwhelming. "Why the hell is she working so hard on the quarry thing if she's supposed to be avoiding stress?"

Caleb looked at him like he'd asked a stupid question. "Because her husband was being treated like a traitor for something he didn't even do, and because she wanted to be part of the solution. Sitting around and doing nothing doesn't make things less stressful, you know."

It hit Peter then. None of this was real, to him. It was a process, a challenge, a game. He'd been proud of himself earlier for reminding Caleb that he'd have to stay in town and deal with his neighbors long after Peter had run back to the city, but that realization on Peter's part had been nothing. Caleb had lost his house, his one point of stability and connection; the doctor was being shunned because his parents had dared to sell their property; and Sarah Dean, a woman he barely knew, might lose her baby at least in part because of his actions. How many other lives were being torn apart because of the game he and his company were playing? He turned away from Caleb; he didn't want the other man to see his face as the realization finally hit him.

But Caleb's hand was gentle on his shoulder. "Peter? You okay?"

"How can you stand to be in the same room with me?" That sounded melodramatic, but damn it, it seemed justified. "I come cruising in here, turn everyone's lives upside down... you lost your *home*, for fuck's sake...."

Caleb didn't withdraw his hand. Instead he pulled, gently but insistently, until Peter gave in and turned around. Caleb lifted his other hand to Peter's jaw and just as gently raised his head until he was looking Caleb in the face. "If it weren't you, it would have been somebody else," Caleb said. "Things change; the world moves on. Farms get turned into quarries, because the world needs gravel. We protest; you negotiate; we all play our parts. You can't worry about every single person in the world, can't just freeze time and not change anything for fear of upsetting somebody." His fingers got a little firmer on Peter's chin. "When I came out of the closet, lots of people said I should have just shut up, kept it quiet, not made a fuss. They didn't want things to change, didn't want to have to deal with a new reality. But things *do* change, whether we want them to or not."

"You coming out is *not* the same as me cruising in here and trying to take your gravel."

"Well, obviously it's not the *same*." Caleb grinned. "It's just two examples of change. But, yeah, for some people, they thought I was being selfish or not paying enough attention to their feelings, their vision of what this town should be like. I don't want gravel trucks; they don't want fags." He raised his eyebrows as if daring Peter to challenge the analogy again. When Peter was silent, Caleb continued, more softly. "Some of them thought I was enough of a monster that I deserved to get the shit kicked out of me; they thought I'd learn my lesson if I spent a couple weeks in the hospital, and the town would go back to being the way it was. But they were *wrong*, Peter."

"You're freaking me out, Caleb. Are you saying you think the quarry's a good idea?"

Caleb dropped his hands. "Fuck, no. I'm just saying... I don't know. There's big stories, and there's little stories. You're here for the big story; you can't be expected to care about all our little stories."

Peter had gone from not being able to look at Caleb to not being able to tear his eyes away. "But what if I *do* care, Caleb? What if the little stories seem like they're... what if they start to seem like the big ones?" He sounded like a little kid, he knew, but he trusted Caleb not to make fun of him.

Caleb shook his head gently. "I have no idea, Peter. No idea at all." And now his hands were back, softly gripping the sides of Peter's shirt just above his waist. "But I bet you're going to be able to figure it out. And I really, really want to see what you come up with."

It was amazing, how fast this had happened. Peter had never removed a single piece of his clothing around Caleb, but there was an intimacy, somehow; a feeling that Caleb had a claim on Peter's body. If Caleb wanted to touch Peter, Caleb absolutely had that right. And when Peter bent his head a little, and Caleb raised his chin, their lips met as if they'd been kissing each other twenty times a day for twenty years. Soft, affectionate, and easy. Nothing like the kiss the night before, but exactly what Peter wanted right then. Exactly what he needed. "Thank you," he whispered when they moved apart.

He smiled at Caleb, and despite it all, Caleb smiled back. And that was when Peter realized that, yes, Caleb had a claim on Peter's body. But he also had a claim to every other part of Peter, as well, anytime he wanted. It was frightening, but it was exhilarating too. Peter wondered whether Caleb was willing to give the same rights to Peter, and he wondered how he'd stand it if Caleb wasn't.

CHAPTER TWENTY-THREE

CALEB called the vet. He called Matt and Sarah. He called the Diefenbakers, who agreed to check on the animals for him, since most of the livestock was in the pasture that abutted the Diefenbakers' farm. And he tried to get through to Jayne Blythe, but was only able to leave a message. Apparently the Northern Nightingale was not a fan of cell phones.

Which meant Caleb should head out to the farm. The police had told him he wasn't allowed to go near the house, but he was free to use the shop or the barn. So he could still show Jayne his work, still take her for a walk down to the quarry site, and still do whatever he could to persuade her to rejoin the campaign. They'd have to have lunch in town; that was all. It wasn't a big deal. Except for the part where he'd have to look at the cold, dead remains of his home.

He stood up and headed into the other room. Peter had left him in the privacy of the bedroom for his calls, but Caleb didn't really want privacy. He wanted Peter.

But when he got to the room used as an office, Peter was nowhere in sight. "He's next door," Riva said, nodding in the direction of her bedroom. "He's talking to lawyers, and the head office."

"The head office?"

She looked at him. "You think it's not going to affect the company if one of their field executives is accused of committing arson in the company's interest? They're freaking out, Caleb."

Caleb knew nothing about corporate policies, but, yeah, he could see how that would be a problem. "Is he in trouble? Are they mad at him?"

"They're not thrilled." Then she took pity on him. "It's not your fault. And it's not his, either, and I think they know that, mostly. But it's his job to make things go smoothly, and arson is *not* smooth. Not at all."

"We should point that out to the police, maybe? Make it clear that the company wouldn't have *wanted* this to happen?"

"There's a team of lawyers on the way. They'll deal with the police." She shrugged. "I know it's hard, but I think we need to keep out of it, at least until we're told exactly what to do."

"Penny Mund-Fischer—I called her earlier—she says we should capitalize on this. She says it's perfect. It'll make the company look bad, and they don't want to look bad, so we can use it to get them to back down. She says whoever burned the house down did us a favor." Caleb kept his expression carefully neutral.

Riva shook her head. "They didn't do *you* a favor, Caleb. But Penny's good at the game. She might not be wrong about how to play this."

"I don't want to play games," Caleb said. "I told her no. I told her the company had nothing to do with this, and I didn't want her using lies to make you guys look bad." He sank down on the end of one of the beds. "I'm tired of it all."

"Yeah." She nodded slowly, then said, "So am I." It seemed like she might have more to add, but there was a knock on the outside door and she stood up to see who it was. She peered through the peephole, then turned to Caleb with a puzzled expression. "It's your brother," she said.

Trevor. Caleb stared at the door. He wasn't ready to deal with Trevor. "I don't know how he knew I was here. Can you tell him I'm somewhere else? I'll go into Peter's room."

Riva gave him an assessing look, then nodded. "Okay. I can do that." Caleb wondered how much Peter had told her, if anything, about Trevor's possible role in the fire. He didn't have time to stop and explain, though, and he wasn't sure it made sense to tell her, anyway. So he stepped through the doorway into Peter's bedroom and half closed the door, enough that he wouldn't be seen but could still hear.

Riva opened the door. "Mr. Sinclair," she started, but then she stopped as if she were being cut off.

"Where's Carr?" Trevor demanded, and Caleb could tell that his brother was in the room, past the doorway.

"Peter? You're here for Peter?"

"You think I'm here for you, sweetheart? Yeah, I want to talk to Carr."

"Well...." Riva sounded as uncertain as Caleb felt. "Okay. He's in the next room. I can see if he's available."

Caleb heard the knock on the other adjoining room door, heard Peter's voice, then Riva saying something softly. Then Peter's voice, tighter than Caleb had ever heard it, saying, "Mr. Sinclair. What can I do for you?"

"I need to talk to you. In private. Can you tell your secretary to go in the other room?"

"She's an engineer," Peter corrected.

"Whatever. This is a private conversation."

Caleb wished he could see his brother; he was pretty sure there'd be a difference. Maybe it wasn't meth; maybe just alcohol, but there was something making his voice too sharp, too loud. Caleb didn't know whether that made it easier or harder to excuse his brother's actions.

Peter paused for a long time before finally saying, "Riva, would you mind? As a favor...."

"Sure," she agreed, and Caleb heard the door to the other

room shut firmly.

"What do you want, Trevor?" Peter sounded pretty damned hostile, but Caleb sympathized with both the words and the tone.

"I just wanted to give you a chance," Trevor said, and Caleb heard that sleazy superficial charm Trevor liked to use. "I heard you're the prime suspect in the fire, and I thought I'd give you the opportunity to convince me to keep my mouth shut. I was thinking there would be a *financial* way of convincing me."

Again, Caleb's reaction matched the expression in Peter's voice; this time, they were both confused. "Keep your mouth shut about what?"

Trevor sounded very pleased with himself. "About your offer to me. The whole town knows we've had meetings, but they don't know what we've been talking about. They don't know that you offered me money to burn down my brother's house. Of course, I refused. I'm a law-abiding citizen now. But if the cops are already convinced you're behind it, and then I tell them you tried to hire me... well, I don't think that would look good for you, *or* for the company. So I'm willing to keep my mouth shut about it. For a price."

Peter had to know Caleb was listening; Riva would have told him, and the door to the bedroom was obviously open. And when Peter said, "We never had any conversation like that. I never said anything like that," it felt as if he was talking to Caleb as much as Trevor.

Trevor's laugh was almost a cackle. "Your word against mine, buddy. And why would I lie?"

Caleb couldn't stand there any longer. He pulled the door open and stepped into the office room; he saw surprise on Trevor's face, and concern on Peter's. "Why didn't you go to the police at the time, Trevor? Why didn't you tell me? You thought somebody was conspiring to burn down my fucking house, and you didn't *tell* me? You honestly think anyone's going to believe that, you son of a bitch?"

Trevor looked a little stunned by the rapid change in the situation, but he adjusted quickly. "He's lying, Caleb! Jesus! I didn't tell you because... because I knew you liked him. I thought it would break your heart! I thought I scared him when I told him that if anything happened to the house, I'd go to the cops. I thought that would be enough to get him to back off."

"You're so full of shit, Trevor! *You* did it! You burned down the fucking house!" Caleb felt out of control. He felt like every insult, every slight that he'd swallowed over years and years of dealing with his brother was rising up in his gut. "Do you think I'm going to give you insurance money? Or part of the sale? I'm not going to give you *shit*, Trevor."

And then Peter was there, standing between Caleb and his brother, and it was only then that Caleb realized how close he'd been to violence. He could almost feel the way Trevor's nose would have crunched under his fist, and he was tempted to duck around Peter and experience the reality. But Peter's hands were on him now, soothing and strong, and Peter's voice was coldly dismissive as he half turned his head to say, "Get out of here, Trevor. Now."

Trevor had never been known for his good sense. "This is bullshit," he protested. "These accusations are insane! I was nowhere near the farm last night. Jesus Christ, Caleb, you've finally gone off the deep end."

"Wait," Caleb said. He wasn't sure whether he was talking to Trevor, Peter, or himself. He needed to think for a second, and he looked up at Peter, saw the concern on his face, and managed to pull himself together. "I'm okay," he said quietly, and Peter nodded slowly and stepped to the side. Then Caleb forced himself to look at Trevor. "You weren't at the farm last night. You haven't been out there since... when?"

Trevor frowned. "Since you gave me those shitty noodles with the stir-fry."

"Two nights ago," Caleb said, ignoring the insult to his cooking. If he was honest, the noodles *had* been a bit unpleasant. "That was absolutely the last time you were there. No questions, no doubts."

"Read my lips, Caleb." Trevor spoke in a slow, exaggerated, and totally obnoxious manner. "The last time I was at the house was two nights ago."

Caleb nodded. It was good that Trevor was being an asshole; it made it easier to do what he had to do. He crossed to the doorway Riva had gone through, knocked, and stepped back when the door was opened almost immediately. "Riva," he said. "I hate to drag you into this, but would you mind...." He turned back to his brother. "Trevor, could you just tell Riva when the last time you were at the farm was?"

"This is fucking stupid, Caleb," Trevor said.

"Yeah, okay, but could you tell her anyway?"

Trevor looked at Riva. "The last time I was at the farm was two nights ago, when my useless brother ruined some perfectly good steak by cutting it up with a bunch of fucking vegetables and serving it on top of fucking disgusting noodles."

"The menu's not the important part," Caleb said. He was suddenly overcome with doubt. This was his brother. Trevor had never been exactly affectionate, but he'd never been... well, that wasn't true, he'd been an asshole lots of times. But he was Caleb's brother, the only family he had left. Could Caleb really do this? He looked at Peter, standing still, confused but ready to help, and knew he could. Trevor had tried to drag Peter into this, had tried to blackmail him, and there was no telling what else Trevor might try. Caleb needed to take a stand.

He turned to face his brother. "There's a camera, Trevor. We set it up for the quarry fight. It's halfway up that rotten birch tree, down by the road. Right on the corner of the property. We set it up so it could see the fields, but also so it could see the road. We wanted to show how little traffic there is now, compared to how much there'd be if the gravel trucks started running. So it saves the footage, Trevor. We'll have a clear view of the road last night; a clear view of exactly who went out to the property, and who left. The fire investigators are going to have a really good idea of what time the fire started." He shook his head. Now that it was clear, the fight had gone out of him, and he mostly just felt sad. "The camera's going to show *you*, isn't it, Trevor?"

Trevor shook his head, but that was all. He didn't even put his denial into words. Instead, he stepped closer. "I needed the money, Caleb. And I made sure you weren't home... I made sure you were safe."

"You should call the cops," Riva said. Her voice was firm. "They need to hear this, and they need to see that tape. The sooner Peter is cleared, the better."

Caleb hadn't gotten that far in his planning. He'd wanted Riva as a witness, sure, but that had been... he wasn't sure why that had been. Had he been planning on turning his brother in? His own brother, flesh and blood, and Caleb was going to have him arrested? And he had a criminal record already, so the punishment would be more severe this time.

"You don't have to, Caleb." It was Peter, smiling sadly as if he knew exactly what Caleb was thinking. "There's absolutely no evidence tying me to the arson. There can't be—I had nothing to do with it. So I'll be okay. It'll be a nuisance—"

"It'll be a hell of a lot more than a nuisance, Peter," Riva broke in, but she stopped when Peter looked at her. She stared at him for a long time, and then she smiled. When she spoke, it was as if she and Peter were the only ones in the room. "Hey, Peter. There's a little question I've been asking myself lately. I'm thinking maybe you've got an answer to it?"

He nodded, and smiled at her, and Caleb tried to control the flash of unreasonable jealousy over their closeness. "Yeah," Peter said quietly. "I'm pretty sure I do."

"What the fuck are they talking about, Caleb?" Then Trevor raised his hands. "No, wait. I don't want to know. But you heard him... there's no need to get the cops involved. Cops would be a *bad* idea, little brother."

"Why did you leave the dogs inside, Trevor?" Caleb had imagined them, trapped in the house that had always been their sanctuary, moving restlessly from room to room as the smoke and heat built, trying to find somewhere they'd be safe, trying to find someone to rescue them... trying to find Caleb. He hadn't been there, but Trevor had. Trevor had lit the fire, and then left the dogs to burn. "Why couldn't you just open the damn door and let them outside?"

Trevor nodded vigorously. "I did that for *you*, Caleb! I saw it on the Internet... it's one of the biggest clues that someone's burned down their own place, if the family heirlooms and the pets escape. So they had to stay in, or else it would look bad for you. I did you a *favor*, Caleb."

Looking back later, Caleb was never sure whether Peter hadn't been quick enough to intervene, or whether he just hadn't tried very hard. One way or the other, he didn't get between the brothers this time, and the connection between Caleb's fist and Trevor's nose was just as satisfying as Caleb had thought it would be. It was the first time in a long time that Caleb was happy with how an interaction with his brother turned out.

CHAPTER TWENTY-FOUR

It HAD been hard, but Peter had managed to wait until everything settled down. He'd *wanted* to go running to the cops with Caleb's evidence and Trevor's confession. He'd wanted to rub their noses in his innocence. But he'd meant it when he told Caleb that they didn't have to involve the police. If it was important to Caleb that Trevor not be charged, then Peter could take some heat for a while.

That didn't mean Peter wasn't pretty damned relieved when Caleb insisted it was time for Trevor to take responsibility for his actions. Caleb had called the cops himself, after Peter had separated the struggling brothers and Trevor had stalked out, his threats and curses only somewhat muffled by the hand he was holding over his bleeding nose.

The cops had gone through the whole process again, separate interviews and all, but the tone had been different this time, especially after Caleb had used Peter's laptop to call up the video. Peter had stood there with his arm wrapped around Caleb as they watched Trevor drive up to the house and then speed away twenty minutes later. Caleb had leaned back into Peter, and the contact was already so familiar, so comforting for both of them, that Peter wondered whether they'd somehow stepped into an alternate, time-warped universe. Was it truly only the night before that Caleb had walked away from Peter, stormed across the parking lot, and declared that they should stay apart?

And when something arrived so quickly, did that mean it

could depart just as suddenly? Peter tried not to think about that. He focused on business, talking to the lawyers, calling the head office—doing his job. But was it doing his job when he didn't mention Jayne Blythe's visit to anyone? Caleb had left the motel in the late morning, just after the police had gone; he was off visiting with Jayne Blythe—showing her the farmland, convincing her of his side of things—and Peter was sitting in the office room, doing nothing. The old Peter, if he'd been aware of this situation, would have been planning a counterattack; hell, he probably would have been out at the site looking at the crops himself, and when Jayne and Caleb appeared, old Peter would have casually strolled over to them with a smile and a rebuttal. He would have played the game, and played it well, and an amateur like Caleb would have been left on the damn sidelines.

Peter pushed back from his desk impatiently, and Riva said, "You okay over there?"

"Everything's upside down," he responded. He didn't really know what he meant, but maybe Riva would. For an engineer, she was pretty damn sensitive about emotional stuff.

But she didn't seem to have any answers right then. Instead she said, "I like Caleb."

"You barely know him. *I* barely know him."

"You know him. Not details, but you know the big picture." She pushed her own chair away from her desk and spun around to look at him. "Did I ever tell you that my parents' marriage was arranged? They met each other, like, five times before the wedding. My mom was back in India, and my dad was Canadian, but the son of immigrants. Their parents set it up, and Dad flew over to India to meet her." Riva smiled at him. "They could have called it off. That was always clear, my mom says. Dad flew over so they could check each other out. Get to know the big picture, and make sure they liked the other person enough to go through with it. They've had the last thirty-seven years to figure out the details."

"That's a great story, Riva, but I'm not really thinking about *marriage* at this point. And your grandparents—they arranged a meeting between people who made *sense* together, right? I mean... there's nothing that makes sense between me and Caleb."

"Why, because you don't have the exact same personalities? Because your job has temporarily brought you into conflict with his lifestyle? *Those* are details, Peter. They're not the big picture."

"What are you even arguing for? I mean, what are you saying? What do you want to see happen here?"

She stood up and gracefully crossed the floor to stand in front of him. "Isn't it obvious, Petey? I want you to be happy. That's all."

"And you think I was unhappy before I came here? Before I met Caleb?"

"No." She looked at him thoughtfully. "I think you were happy before meeting him. But I'm not sure you'll be happy *after* meeting him. Not if you walk away from this."

Peter rocked back in his chair and ran his hands roughly through his short hair. "So this has been a bad thing, then. I was happy, and now I might be unhappy. You're saying my meeting Caleb was bad."

Riva laughed. "You should see the face you made when you said that! I think we both know your meeting Caleb wasn't bad." She laid both her hands flat on the sides of his face and tilted his head more to her liking. She looked at him critically and said, "Nope. Not bad." She leaned forward quickly and kissed his forehead. "But scary. I get that. That's the problem with asking questions. Sometimes, you figure out the answer."

"For the record," Peter said, his voice only a little distorted by her hands on his cheeks, "I wasn't the one asking the questions. That was you. So I don't know why *I* have to sort out all this crap, just because *you* had some sort of super-early midlife crisis."

She straightened up and smiled. "Because we're partners, sahib. You're stuck with me."

He caught her wrist just as she was withdrawing her hand. "Even if we change jobs? Even if... I don't know, if you do that thing you were talking about, where you settle down and cook and clean for your new hubby... even if I do something different... we're still partners, right?"

"Never doubt it. You're stuck with me." She smiled fondly at him, then released herself from his loose grip and went back to her desk. But when she sat down she was still facing him, as if waiting for more.

And apparently she was right; he wasn't quite done talking yet. "I'm thinking... some fairly drastic thoughts. In terms of the job. This project, at least; maybe not the job as a whole. I don't know. I need to sort some ideas out. I just don't want any of it to affect you. If I go down in flames, I want to be sure you're clear of the fire."

She frowned at him. "Terrible metaphor, Peter. I was in your room earlier, and I smelled the smoke on your clothes. You had a close call, and I really don't need to be reminded of it." She sounded genuinely upset.

"Okay, sorry. I just... I'm maybe going to be sailing through stormy seas, and I don't want you to be... dragged into the whirlpool? Does that work?" He paused. "Also, stop smelling my clothes, you pervert."

"I didn't have a choice, asshole; the whole room reeked." But she was laughing, at least. "Don't worry about me. I can chart my own course."

"And you will? You won't do some loyalty thing, where you think you need to stand by me even if I'm doing something really stupid?"

"Don't flatter yourself, buddy. I will drop you in a hot second, just as soon as you are no longer of use to me."

"Seriously... you should. I mean, you have yourself to look after, and I don't know *what* the hell I'm doing, so... you are officially released of any and all responsibility toward me or my career. Okay?"

Another smile. "You just can't let me win, can you? If I have a little bit of doubt about my professional direction, you have to have a huge career crisis. If I ask a little question about the completeness of our lives, you have to answer it with a... well, I don't know what we're calling this, exactly. But it's big, whatever it is."

He couldn't argue with that. Whatever this was, whatever he was feeling for Caleb, whatever he was feeling about himself... yeah, it was big. He stood up decisively. "I'm going to call the office," he declared. "I shouldn't mess around on this."

Riva looked at him thoughtfully. "I think the responsible thing for me to do would to be tell you to slow down and not jump into anything. I think I should remind you that there's no rush; nobody's pushing you to make any decisions right away."

He waited. "So... *are* you going to remind me of all that?" He was pretty sure he wasn't going to listen, if she did. He was loyal to his company; loyal enough to think it was his duty to let them know if one of their employees was off his game. That didn't change just because *he* happened to be the slacking worker. But if Riva had something to say, he respected her enough to hear her out.

But she just gave him another one of her beatific smiles. "No, I don't think I am," she said. "You haven't got any dependents for me to worry about, and you and Scott get along so well that if you show up on my doorstep in four months, unemployed and homeless, it won't be a big problem for me to loan you a bed." She leaned back in her chair. "I think I'm just going to watch this one play out. I'm really enjoying the show so far."

"I'm glad you're entertained," he said, and he started for the door to his bedroom. He stopped partway there. "He could dump me tomorrow," he told her. "I mean, he kind of dumped me already, last night. Things have changed, but still... there is absolutely no guarantee here."

She leaned forward and whispered, "I know! That's what makes it fun!" Then she leaned back and her face got more serious. "Whatever decision you're making, Peter, ask yourself: Are you doing it for Caleb, or are you doing it for you?"

It was a good question, and the more Peter thought about it, the clearer everything became. "Thanks, Riva. And, you know, when you finally catch up to me and have your own career meltdown, I'll be there for you. And I'll be living in your guest room, probably, so... it'll be pretty convenient."

"I look forward to it," she said, and he grinned at her before he headed into the other room to make his call.

CHAPTER TWENTY-FIVE

CALEB had only met Jayne Blythe once before. It had been at a gallery opening for a studio that was featuring functional art, and he'd had a few pieces on display. It had been a big, ritzy party, and he'd felt totally out of place. But he'd met Jayne. She'd been ebullient and complimentary and larger than life; he'd assumed she was drunk.

He was reassessing that conclusion now, because it was barely past noon, she'd been with him for over an hour and he hadn't seen her take a drop to drink, and she was at least as out of control as she'd been at the gallery. In a fun way, but still... it was exhausting. First, she'd commiserated with him over the ashes of his house. From a distance, as there was still yellow caution tape all around the blackened shell, and some crime-scene technicians still scurried around gathering evidence. Then she'd spent more time than he would have thought possible in the shop, going on and on about his process, and his vision, and his legacy. The last one had creeped him out a little, made him feel as if she was waiting for him to die so she could sell his work at a premium. But it had all been said with such innocent enthusiasm that it was difficult to take offense.

And it had been nice to have her there so he didn't have time to focus on the quite literal ashes of his previous life. As he helped her into the passenger seat of his truck for the ride into town, he let himself take one quick look at the house and then hurried around to the driver's side. Everything was destroyed. Even the front of the house, built of stone, was toppled and crooked; it looked as if falling beams from the ceiling and roof had knocked into the walls. He would go back, he supposed, once the police gave him the all clear, but he could tell he wouldn't be doing much more than cleaning up. There was nothing to salvage, and little reason to rebuild.

"Maybe you'll settle somewhere else now," Jayne said as he steered the truck down the driveway. "You could, you know. If you came up to Toronto, I could introduce you to some lovely people. It'd be so much easier for you to find a market for your work, and you could be part of the artistic community. Galleries and museums, maybe even collaborations with other people who inspire you. When I was singing, I was always at my best when I worked with the best people. They gave me energy."

It was hard to imagine Jayne having any sort of energy shortage, and Caleb smiled. Then he thought of Peter, saying almost the same thing. He got his energy from meeting with people, working the crowd. Peter, who lived in Toronto. Caleb didn't want to give up the fight against the quarry, but maybe it was time for him to think about giving up his fight against leaving the area. He could fight just as well, if not better, from the city. He was probably being foolish, imagining he could keep Peter's attention for any length of time, but maybe he'd try, anyway. Even if he couldn't have Peter, maybe he owed it to himself to try to find *somebody*, instead of living the rest of his life as a hermit. "Maybe," he said to Jayne. She blinked at him as if she no longer had any idea what he was responding to, but she didn't seem too worried, and kept up a steady stream of chatter as Caleb guided them down the familiar road into town.

What would it be like not to drive that road anymore? The oaks at the Aiken place, little twigs when he and Mike Witmore had planted them as a weekend job, were now up over his head—what would it be like not to see them grow any taller? The creek just this side of town, where he and Matt still sometimes took fishing poles during trout season—he supposed the fish wouldn't miss him much, but he was pretty sure he'd miss them. And Matt himself, and Sarah... and the baby they would, surely, someday have, one way or another. Caleb had liked the thought of being an honorary uncle, using his flexible work schedule to help out when the new parents needed a sitter. It would be hard to do that from Toronto.

But... Peter. Warm smiles, strong arms, and passion. Didn't Caleb deserve that? Didn't he at least deserve a chance?

He pulled into the diner parking lot. He'd consulted with Sarah, and they'd agreed that the diner was the best option, even though it wasn't a great one. The décor was utilitarian, but the food was, while not fancy, at least presentable. Sarah had dropped by the shop earlier and promised to get a few other committee members together for lunch, so Caleb wouldn't have to carry the conversation himself. Not that he was having too much trouble with that, he realized; he'd barely said a word on the whole drive in, and he wasn't sure Jayne had noticed.

He slipped out of his seat and circled around to open the door for Jayne. She'd been surprisingly agile and easygoing when they'd walked down to look at the quarry site, but now she was back in civilization and obviously expected to be treated like a lady. Caleb was happy to oblige, and even gave her a bit of a boost down from the truck's high seat. She patted his arm like a fond grandmother and then arranged him the way she wanted, with her hand resting on the crook of his elbow. He felt like a little kid playing dress-up, but he didn't protest.

She disengaged herself when he had to hold the diner door open for her, and she swept inside as if going onstage to accept a standing ovation. It only surprised Caleb a little when the patrons offered a round of applause. Sarah had obviously done a good job rounding people up. It sounded like Jayne had a full, appreciative house.

Caleb was a bit confused when Jayne stood aside and gestured for him to precede her into the room, and the applause didn't stop. She seemed to think the crowd was clapping for

Caleb, and that was incredibly embarrassing.

He ducked behind her a little, and then bent down to frantically whisper, "They're excited to see you. They're clapping for you!"

She smiled as she shook her head. "No, dear boy, they're not."

And then Sarah was there, holding her hands up for silence as she addressed the crowd. "Here they are, our guests of honor! Please allow me to introduce Ms. Jayne Blythe, the Northern Nightingale herself, and our own Caleb Sinclair, who's been the driving force behind the anti-quarry movement, and whose beautiful table has inspired bids from all over the world in our fundraising auction. The latest bid is for thirty-two *thousand* dollars from someone in Dubai!" Sarah beamed at him, then turned back to the crowd. "We all know that Caleb's run into some trouble at home, and I want to thank you all for coming out today for this fundraising luncheon. The house was insured, but insurance never covers everything." She looked over at Caleb then, and smiled as she said, "And, as I have learned since I became part of the Rocky Creek community, we look after our own."

Caleb wasn't sure whether Sarah was forgetting about the way the town had turned on her husband, or whether she was using her praise to make their betrayal even more poignant. Either way, it was hard for him to accept her words without at least a little cynicism. Then he looked out at the crowd. Carrie Ross was in the front row with her husband Dave; they ran the town's only garage, and had always been honest and friendly with Caleb when his truck needed repairs. Will and Martha Cogburn were sitting by the window with their three almost grown sons, and Caleb remembered the first time he'd gotten drunk; he'd been stumbling home from a field party and Will had picked him up at the side of the road, taken him back to the Cogburn house, and gotten him clean and sober before dropping him off at his grandparents' the next day. Mrs. Solomon was there, Caleb's eighth-grade teacher. She'd been the first one to congratulate him when he'd come out, and she'd crossed the street on a windy February day to do it.

There were others. So many others. People he'd grown up with, people who'd seen him at his best and worst, and who had always treated him as one of their own. He turned to Sarah, and softly said, "Most of the town kept going to see Matt. There were a few people who were cruel, but most of them... most of them understood."

She smiled at him. "Yeah, most of them did." She didn't say the rest, because she didn't have to. She didn't need to tell him that most of the town had been just fine with him all along as well. And then, because she was Sarah and she knew him, she turned back to the waiting crowd. "Caleb's had a long couple days and I expect he needs to sit down and have some lunch, but I had the chance to sneak a few words with Ms. Blythe earlier today, and she has generously offered to treat us to a few songs while we enjoy our meal. Tina Manelli has agreed to accompany her." Sarah gestured over to a corner table where the high-school music teacher had set up a portable keyboard and some speakers.

Under cover of the crowd's applause, Sarah led Caleb to a table near the front of the room, where Matt was waiting with a few other guys Caleb had grown up with. It had been a long time since he'd seen them, and he realized they weren't the ones who'd stopped calling after he came out; it had been the other way around.

Tommy Baker raised a glass of water in his direction. "Damn, Caleb, you were always good in shop class, but $32,000? I should have been taking notes."

"You should have at least shown up," Phil Markton said. "Have a seat, Caleb. My parents are back there somewhere, and I swear, they're gonna die of happiness-induced heart attacks from getting to hear Jayne Blythe sing live. Good work, man."

Caleb sat. He wasn't sure why he was being praised. For

making a table? For asking Jayne Blythe to come to town? None of it made sense, and it all felt totally surreal. But maybe he didn't care. Maybe, for a few minutes, he'd let himself sit back and enjoy the affection, without questioning its veracity or doubting its source.

Jayne Blythe spoke into the microphone she'd been handed. Sarah had been heard through the room without trouble, but Ms. Blythe wasn't as young as she used to be, and Sarah had the volume control of an elementary school teacher. "It's a pleasure to be here in Rocky Creek," Jayne said warmly. "And a pleasure to see a community coming together to support one of its own. I've got to tell you... Caleb took me out to that quarry site this morning, and that is some fine, fine land. I really do think it would be a shame to see it wasted on a hole in the ground, and I think we all need to keep working to make sure that doesn't happen."

The crowd applauded. Everyone smiled, and Caleb smiled too. It was good news, a victory for his cause. But he thought of Peter, and he wondered whether the good news in the diner was going to be bad news for someone else.

CHAPTER TWENTY-SIX

DIESEL must still be pretty heavily drugged, Peter decided. Diego had greeted him warmly, if a little dopily, but Diego was happy to see *everybody*. Diesel, on the other hand—Diesel had actually half wagged his tail when Peter stood in front of his cage and said hello. And the only way that made sense was if Diesel was stoned.

Peter leaned a little closer to the bars of the cage before whispering, "Don't bogart the good shit, dude. We could all stand to take the edge off...."

And damn if the dog didn't wag his tail again, a single lift of the muscular appendage followed by a heavy thump as it fell to the floor of the cage.

"I need to film this," Peter said. "You are going to be *so* embarrassed when you sober up."

"I said you should talk to them, not taunt them," the pretty veterinary assistant said from behind him. She sounded amused. "It's supposed to help keep them calm, not enrage them."

"Diesel's not enraged," Peter said. "He's got a good sense of himself. He's not going to worry about what some puny human thinks. Right, Diesel?" Peter was tempted to reach his fingers through the bars and give good ol' Diesel a little ear rub, but the still-sore tooth holes on his hand reminded him not to press his luck.

"You're not going over to the diner?" the assistant asked. "Half the town's over there. Dr. Rivkin took his lunch early so he could go over first, and then he's going to come back and cover for me so I can go over. They say Jayne Blythe is there, and she's going to sing!"

The assistant couldn't be over twenty-five, and Peter looked at her quizzically. "You a big fan of Jayne Blythe?"

She shrugged. "Not, like, a *fan*, but she's super famous. My grandparents *love* her." She gave him a look. "This isn't Toronto, you know. We don't get big-name acts down here. Jayne Blythe is *huge*."

Yeah. She was. And it was huge that she seemed to be back on the anti-quarry team. Peter felt a surge of competitive energy. Was he good enough? Could he still get this back? This was just the sort of challenge that brought out the best in him. Would he challenge Blythe directly? He could go negative if he had to, and point out the hypocrisy of her position. She lived in a big house, with lots of concrete, but nobody *else* could have gravel? That would be risky, to take on a beloved icon that way. Maybe he'd take a mock compassionate approach, thanking her for trying to stay on top of events while making it crystal clear she didn't know what she was talking about. A little more subtle, but still not exactly his style. He'd built a career out of being reasonable, and decent—and smart, for sure, but not a smart*ass*. Besides, it wasn't playing to his main strength. No, if he was going to do this, he'd do it right. He'd get on the job and out-charm the crazy old bird, *that's* what he'd do.

"*That's* what I'd do, Diesel, my buddy."

"He's your buddy now?" The voice from behind him was more familiar than it had any right to be after such a short time. "He bites you, and now you're friends?" Caleb came to the bars of the cage and fearlessly stuck his hand inside to be greeted with friendly, if somewhat sloppy, licks. Diego struggled closer to the bars of his own cage, and Caleb reached in to greet him, as well. "They're doing okay?"

"The vet said he was pleased. Wants to keep monitoring

them, but he's taking them off the sedation. Diego more than Diesel, obviously." Peter was strangely, suddenly nervous, like a high school kid talking to his first crush. "I hope it's okay that I came to visit them. I was kind of at loose ends, and I just thought I'd check in." And then he frowned. "What are *you* doing here? Isn't there a big party over at the diner? Isn't it kind of in your honor?"

"I'm not good at that sort of thing," Caleb said quietly. "And I wanted to check on the dogs." Then he looked straight at Peter for the first time since he'd arrived. "And Dr. Rivkin said you were here."

"Oh." Peter nodded slowly. "I am."

Now it was Caleb's turn to look nervous. "I'm not... I'm not saying this is something it isn't. I just thought I'd check in." He took a deep breath as if forcing himself to continue. "And, you know, I'd like it if it was something. Us. If we were something. I'd like to, you know... see where that goes. If you're still into it." Another deep breath, and this time he seemed to be using it to force himself to stop talking.

Peter looked down at the spot where Caleb's fingers disappeared into the thick fur of Diesel's ruff. "I took a leave from my job," he said. "I was maybe going to quit, but they talked me into taking a leave." He looked up quickly. "Not for you. Not... I mean, kind of for you, but for me too, you know? I've been... well, actually, *Riva*'s been questioning stuff lately, and it's kind of contagious. I thought I should try to reassess a few things. See where I was, and where I wanted to go." And then he decided it was time to push his luck. "But I know where I am—I'm here, with you. And I don't seem to have any damn interest in going anywhere else."

Peter had been so busy looking at Caleb's face that he hadn't noticed the other man's hands moving, not until Caleb wrapped the strong fingers of one hand around the back of Peter's neck and pulled his head down. The kiss was almost desperate, as if

Caleb wanted, *needed* Peter to understand a secret message. And with a warm wash of relief and affection, Peter realized he *did* understand. "We're going to try this, right?"

Caleb nodded fervently. "Damn right we are."

"We're going to make it work, Caleb."

Another nod, this one slower but no less sincere. "Yeah. Okay." And then he was smiling, his happiness an almost visible light shining from him. "Yeah. We are."

"Do the dogs need you? Or can we get out of here? Maybe go back to the motel...."

"Dr. Rivkin said the dogs should sleep for a while. They'll be fine." Caleb frowned. "But... not the motel. I don't... I mean, it's fine, but it's not...."

It wasn't. But they were pretty low on options.

"The cops are done at my house," Caleb said. "I can go back whenever I want to and start looking through the rubble."

Okay, maybe Caleb had a totally different idea of what their next step should be. Peter didn't want to be crude, but.... "There's no... there's no bed there. There's no *house* there, Caleb. Not anymore."

Caleb shook his head in what Peter hoped was mock disappointment. "You city boys. You're all about the beds, and the buildings. In the country, we're a little more creative." His smirk was a dare Peter was happy to take.

"I'm in your hands, then, country boy. Show me your wicked ways."

Caleb nodded, then turned and headed out the door toward the front office. Peter followed wordlessly. He wasn't sure where they were going or exactly what they were going to do when they got there, but he didn't much care. He was going to be with Caleb, and that was enough for him.

Chapter Twenty-seven

CALEB'S confidence deserted him about halfway down the short flight of steps from the vet's office, but he refused to give up. The whole thing was a gamble, a shot in the dark, so why should this detail be any different?

He made it to his truck and slid behind the wheel as Peter climbed in on the passenger side. It was different, being the one driving, but Caleb liked it.

He barely noticed any of the landmarks that had seemed so important on his drive into town. He was still uncertain about his future, still didn't know if he'd see the Aikens' oak trees mature, but none of that seemed to matter, not compared to the growing, driving needs of his body. It had been too long since he'd been with anybody, and he'd *never* wanted anyone the way he wanted Peter Carr.

He glanced nervously across the cab at Peter, who saw his look and responded with a slow, sly smile. Peter stretched his long body as far as he could in his seat, a long, languorous line of muscular flesh, and when he returned to a relaxed position, his hand was resting gently, almost possessively, on the growing bulge in his jeans. Caleb wasn't sure whether to slow down to increase his chance of staying on the road despite his distraction, or speed up so he could get his hands on Peter faster. When Peter's fingers spread out and slowly started stroking along his own fly, Caleb floored it.

They skidded to a halt in a spray of gravel, and Caleb had

his door open before the engine had fully stopped. He leaned dangerously, tantalizingly close to Peter in order to open the glove box, and it was only the promise of future pleasure that allowed him to maintain any sort of focus on his task. It had seemed like the height of optimism months earlier when he'd stocked the truck with condoms and lube, but now he blessed his foresight. Once he had what he needed he shut the glove box and pulled the dog blanket out from its cubbyhole, trying not to think too hard about the last time it had been washed.

"Come on," he said, and the voice he heard barely seemed like his own. Since when did he sound so husky, so simultaneously confident and desperate? But Peter was moving to follow him, so Caleb didn't have time for further analysis.

He headed back past the outbuildings, through the orchard, and into the forest. He knew exactly where they were going. The clearing was on high ground, so the soil was relatively dry, and it was far enough from the house that it was protected from view. It was also one of Caleb's favorite spots on the property, and he wanted to share it with Peter.

But when they arrived, Peter didn't seem interested in admiring the scenery. He managed to stand still while Caleb hastily spread the blanket, but then he was *there*, his rangy body surrounding Caleb, making him feel owned and cherished and safe. Peter's lips were hard against Caleb's, his tongue demanding entrance as if returning to its own home, and Caleb gave no thought to objecting as Peter's hands roamed over Caleb's body freely, claiming and then exploring their new possession.

Peter tugged Caleb's shirt up impatiently, pulled it over his head, and then froze with the fabric still bunched around Caleb's arms. "Trust me?" he asked, his eyes hot and intent on Caleb's.

Caleb wasn't sure what Peter was asking, exactly, but he knew what his answer was. "Yeah," he breathed, and Peter lowered his head to Caleb's chest, kissed him just over his heart, and trailed kisses down to Caleb's nipples, then farther. Peter paused when he got to Caleb's straining fly, and Caleb shifted, trying to make himself more obviously available. That was when he realized his shirt was still partway on, holding his arms behind his back. When he tried to wriggle free, he found that Peter had knotted the fabric, trapping Caleb's wrists.

"You want loose?" Peter asked. Caleb didn't doubt that an affirmative answer would result in an instant release of the bonds. Which meant he didn't need to worry about it.

"No, I'm fine." He grinned. "I guess you city boys have a few tricks of your own, huh?"

Peter smiled back at him, and kept their gazes locked as his long, elegant fingers eased open the buttons of Caleb's fly. Caleb wanted to close his eyes; it was too much, too perfect to see Peter there, hovering over the only part of Caleb that seemed to matter right then, looking up and waiting... for what?

"Please," Caleb said. He wasn't sure if that was what Peter had wanted or if it was just enough of a prompt to call Peter back to himself, but it worked. Peter slid his hand down inside Caleb's underwear, and Caleb's whole body jerked forward when Peter's fingers wrapped around their target. Then it all happened fast. Somehow, Peter managed to get rid of Caleb's pants, and his mouth was on Caleb's cock, softly at first, but then harder, more demanding. Suction, friction, wet and warmth; it was all perfect, intoxicating, irresistible. "Peter, I'm going to...." Caleb tried, because he didn't want this to be over, wanted to do more and more and more. But he couldn't say any of that because his body took over, his hips driving forward, deeper into Peter's mouth, into his throat. Caleb's excitement seemed to inspire Peter to new heights, and the flicker of his tongue increased in speed and pressure until it felt like there was a soft, wet vibrator working the underside of Caleb's cock.

He couldn't last. He heard his muffled cry as if he were far away, and his whole body convulsed as his awareness funneled down to the one spot where his body was joined with Peter's.

Peter worked him through his orgasm and seemed to know the exact moment when the stimulation became too much. He abandoned Caleb's cock with a final, regretful kiss, then straightened up.

"I'm sorry," Caleb started to say, but Peter stopped him with a strong, deep kiss.

When Peter pulled away, he was smiling. "You only good for one round, country boy? 'Cause now that I've got you all tied up and right where I want you... I'm thinking I'd like to stick around for a while."

CHAPTER TWENTY-EIGHT

CALEB's body was addictive. Peter wanted to explore every nook and cranny, wanted to taste every inch of skin. And once he'd been over it all once, he found that he wanted to do it again. And again. He'd lost track of time, barely even remembered where they were... all he cared about was Caleb's body, the way it felt beneath his hands, the way it responded to his touch. He wanted to *own* Caleb, wanted to make it clear to their bodies, at least, that this wasn't just a fling. And, yeah, he'd like to come at some point reasonably soon, but that wasn't his most pressing need.

No; what he really needed was to hear Caleb moan again. They were stretched out on the rough blanket, Caleb's hands still loosely bound behind him, his cock already hard again. Peter ran his hands down Caleb's strong back, slipped his thumbs into the lubed cleft of Caleb's ass where they'd already been so many times before, and felt Caleb's hips tilt in response as he wantonly offered himself to Peter. That was good. It was damn near perfect, and Peter's cock throbbed with the need to take advantage of the situation. But Peter wanted to hear that moan, just once more.

He leaned down and ran his stubble over Caleb's shoulders, finding the spot on Caleb's neck where he'd already left his mark. Another nip, more hard suction, and Caleb gasped, breathy and desperate and wonderful. But it wasn't the moan.

He slid his hand under Caleb's shoulder and rolled him over onto his back, then threw a leg across so he was straddling the smaller man, their cocks lined up, hard and leaking and ready. Peter wrapped his hand around both erections, grip almost too tight, and shifted his hips gently, rocking into his hand and against Caleb's cock. That earned him another gasp, and then, as Peter increased the pressure just a little, he heard it: the desperate, hungry moan he craved.

He already had the condom on; he'd been teasing Caleb's hole with his cock for quite a while. But now he was ready. He was more than ready; he was desperate. He lifted Caleb's legs and held them with his shoulders, then ran his hands over Caleb's calves, his thighs, and back to Caleb's ass. They'd already done this before, too, and as Peter lined up, he knew Caleb expected more teasing.

"Please, Peter. Fuck me. Just fucking...." And then Peter pushed inside, deep and hard, and Caleb's voice became almost a scream as he threw his head back and accepted Peter into his body. "God, yeah. Oh, God, Peter, that's perfect, that's...." Caleb's babbling stopped when Peter started to move. Slow, deep thrusts, pushing until he was in to the hilt and then pushing a little more, rocking Caleb back, then dragging him forward as Peter withdrew, before rocking him back again. Caleb's hands were bound, but the knot was loose enough that he could reach the sides of his body, and Peter watched his fingers clenching and releasing in time with Peter's thrusts.

As Peter's tempo increased, so did the volume of Caleb's encouragement. He stopped using words after a while, and eventually it was just nonsense syllables being practically shouted into the distant blue sky. Shy, quiet Caleb, losing control because of Peter. It was intoxicating and glorious, and Peter let the sounds wash over his body like a baptism.

He could feel Caleb's body tightening even as his own orgasm approached. He wanted more, but he didn't want to risk changing the angle at which they were joined. So instead of bending his own body to find Caleb's, he reached down and wrapped his fingers around Caleb's neck, pulling him up for a gasping, distracted kiss. Peter felt the orgasm rip through Caleb's body and tried to watch, tried to memorize the beauty of the moment, but his body betrayed him, sending him hurtling after Caleb with his eyes shut and his mind blank of everything but ecstasy.

He let himself fall to rest on Caleb's chest, and their kiss now was softer, sweeter, and less desperate.

"I like this outdoor thing," Peter said, once his breath and his composure returned.

"You won't like it once the sweat cools. We're going to get cold out here; it's only April."

"Warm, for April," Peter said with a yawn.

"Cold, for naked."

"You're not naked. You've still got your shirt on." Peter ran his hands back along Caleb's bound arms. Damn. He liked that. Liked thinking that he had the man contained, unable to escape.

"You planning on letting me loose?" Caleb asked. He sounded fairly nonchalant about it.

"No," Peter said seriously. "I might take the shirt off, or put it back on properly, if you want me to. But no, Caleb... I'm not planning on letting you loose."

Caleb looked serious, as if he understood and appreciated all that Peter was trying to say. Finally, he leaned over for a kiss. "Good," he said when he pulled away. "Because I'm not planning on letting you loose, either."

So Peter sorted out Caleb's shirt, and they got dressed, and Caleb buried the condom under some rotting leaves.

"You're part druid, aren't you?" Peter asked. "This whole thing has been like a... a fertility rite, sacrificing the seed of a virile young man to ensure a fruitful harvest in the upcoming year."

"Damn, you figured out my secret." Caleb leaned in close,

teasing and seductive, then grabbed the front of Peter's shirt in a surprisingly tight grip. "But it doesn't last for the entire year. If we want this to work, I'm going to need to have my way with you every damn day through the entire growing season."

"Wow. That's quite a sacrifice. But I know how important the farmland is to you, so... I'll try to help out."

Caleb grinned and released Peter's shirt. "That's cute, you acting like you have a choice." Then he got more serious, and he ran his hand down Peter's arm until their fingers met and twined together. "We've still got a couple hours of light. I want to go look at the house. See if there's anything... you know. Anything to save."

Damn. It was easy to forget it, in the excitement of this new... relationship, Peter supposed he could legitimately call it now... but Peter shouldn't let himself. The last twenty-four hours had cost Caleb his home and what was left of his family, and he was going to have to come to terms with it. "Do you want privacy, or company? I'm fine with either, but if you're on the fence... cast my vote for company. I'd like to be there with you."

Caleb nodded solemnly. "I'd like that too." He gave a quick grin as he added, "I think there's going to be some heavy lifting, and I need all the muscle I can get."

It seemed so natural, so casual. Peter felt like his world had been shifting on its axis in sudden jolts for too long. Riva's questions, meeting Caleb, taking a leave from his job, and then, just moments earlier, joining, claiming, possessing Caleb with more intensity than Peter had ever imagined. And now, they were talking and joking and going to clean up a sooty mess. It was unsettling. But when Caleb started walking, Peter fell in behind him. Maybe this was what it was like. Maybe Peter wasn't used to feeling unsettled because he wasn't used to caring. He'd spent a lifetime skimming over the surface of life, but now he was diving deep, and finding turbulence and an undertow. But he was also finding beauty he'd never known existed.

"I was thinking about your trees," he said, and Caleb stopped walking and turned to look at him. "Your story. About how your great-great-grandparents had cut the trees down, and burned them in the fireplace, and then spread the ashes back in the forest. And then the saplings soaked up the nutrients and grew big and strong, and they got cut down and burned, and their ashes were spread, and then they grew again...." He wasn't sure if this was useful or not, but Caleb was still listening, so he kept going. "I know it doesn't make up for everything you lost. But I was thinking, you know... you didn't really *lose* all of it. Right? We can spread the ashes in the forest, if you want. Or we could plant some trees right there on the site, if you decide you don't want to rebuild, or don't want to build in the same spot." This was starting to sound a bit stupid. "I guess it takes trees a long time to grow, huh? I mean, it's not like you could build your new place with the trees that grow from those ashes. Not unless you wait a hell of a long time." He started walking again, but Caleb caught his arm.

"Not me," Caleb agreed, but he smiled. "But maybe my kids, or my grandkids. Maybe they'll build an addition to a house I build. Or maybe one of them will work with wood, and will cut down the trees and build something beautiful from them. Something that's connected to their family history for generation after generation." He nodded slowly. "It helps, Peter. It really does. Thank you." Then he grinned. "It's all part of the process, right?"

"Well," Peter said, "now that you mention it...."

Caleb laughed and took his hand, and Peter held on tight. He was walking an unknown path, with no idea of his destination. But he was traveling with the person he wanted to be with, and he was looking forward to the adventure.

Epilogue

Peter was winning, damn it. The bastard was good. Too good. He had more experience at this, Caleb told himself, and he was a people person, born and bred to manipulate emotional responses. Caleb tried not to groan as Peter stretched his whole body, his bare arms reaching almost to the condo ceiling, his shoulder muscles rolling and bunching under smooth, tanned skin. The bastard was pretty good at manipulating *physical* response too.

It was time for desperate measures. Caleb reached his finger into the cream cheese on his plate and smeared a little out on his cheek, right next to the spot Peter called his baby dimple. Of course, that gambit would only work if Peter turned his fine ass around and *looked* at Caleb. They'd never really formalized the rules of this little game, but Caleb was pretty sure it was cheating if one person never even *looked* at the other. He needed to draw Peter's attention.

"I talked to the contractor," he tried. "He says they're still on track for completion mid-October. We should be in there before the snow flies."

Peter nodded absentmindedly. "Penny says she's got work for me until Christmas. But I should be able to do a lot of it from down there. Teleconferencing, writing, whatever. Same as I'm doing here, really." He half turned, so the midmorning sun caught the highlights in his hair and made them glow. He rubbed at his chest as if unconscious of doing it, and Caleb felt a rush of desire. He was touching the marks Caleb had left on him the night before. Savoring them. The bastard was kicking Caleb's ass, and the cream cheese wasn't doing one bit of good.

Caleb's weak will and lustful nature had cost him the game the past three Sundays in a row, and he would *not* allow himself to be defeated again. He decided to go in for the close-up. It was risky. Proximity might tempt Peter, but it would make it more difficult for Caleb to resist, as well. Peter's hand slid lower on his torso, still just absentmindedly rubbing his skin, and Caleb knew he had to act fast.

He stood up and headed for the window. His pajama shirt was open, showing just a flash of his chest; that had certainly been an effective lure in the past. And maybe he could figure out a reason to make a few sounds... that always got Peter worked up fast. He grabbed the last half bagel as he left the table, and wished the melted cheese on it was a little hotter, a little gooier. Still, maybe Peter wouldn't realize that.

Caleb brushed by Peter, just barely touching him. Touching, he was pretty sure, was totally against the rules. But brushing? Brushing was a judgment call. He thought about mentioning Trevor, but immediately decided against it. At some point he'd want to talk to Peter about that, want to discuss the defense lawyer's request that Caleb speak up for his brother. But not now. Not on Sunday morning, with the sun shining in and Peter looking so beautiful. Thinking about Trevor made Caleb sad, and that made Peter... well, different things. Sometimes angry, sometimes sad, sometimes just frustrated. None of those were emotions that Caleb wanted to allow into his Sunday morning.

He perched on the window seat, one leg bent so he could rest his elbow on his knee, the other trailing down to where Diego was lying on the floor, hoping for dropped scraps. The dogs weren't crazy about condo living, but they definitely appreciated having two humans to "accidentally" feed them people food. And Caleb still spent a few days a week down at his shop, so they got to run around then. When Caleb was in Toronto, working with the architects and designers Jayne

Blythe had introduced him to, the dogs had to settle for their morning run with Peter and their evening walk with both men.

But the dogs were a distraction. Caleb needed to keep his head in the game. "They've got the foundation laid," he said. He hoped there'd be some subliminal effect from the word *laid*, but Peter seemed oblivious, all his attention focused on the sailboats on Lake Ontario.

"For the house?" Peter asked. "They had that done three weeks ago."

"No, for the processing plant. It's right where you suggested it be, by the highway."

"So it'll be ready for next year's crop?" Peter finally seemed interested in Caleb's news. He'd worked so hard to stay neutral on the quarry fight, trying to support Caleb without betraying his employer's trust, and sometimes he still forgot that he was *allowed* to talk about it now. It had been mostly his idea, after all. When the quarry opposition had been at its strongest, Peter had suggested that they needed to give the company some way out, some way to still make a reasonable profit from the land and not make it look like they were backing down. Penny Mund-Fischer, Peter's new boss, had suggested that they go back to the crop the Deans had thought the company was going to grow: ginseng. But there wasn't enough money in that to make it tempting, not until Peter had started leaving articles around the condo, studies showing that the vast majority of Canada's ginseng crop was exported to China for processing before being distributed worldwide. The terms of Peter's resignation from his old job had made it clear that he wasn't allowed to have anything to do with any aspect of the company's projects, but Peter was a fixer, and couldn't stand aside and watch things not work. Caleb still smiled when he thought of Peter's attempt to look surprised by Caleb's proposal for the company to build a processing plant on a small portion of the farmland, leaving the rest for growing the ginseng itself.

But thinking of Peter being adorably bad at lying was not helping Caleb with the contest. Damn it. He took a bite of the bagel and let out a little moan, as if overwhelmed by the deliciousness of the congealed cheddar. It wasn't a good effort, but it was enough to catch Peter by surprise. He glanced over at Caleb, and then broke out laughing.

"What?" Caleb demanded. This was not going according to plan at *all.*

"Caleb, baby... food on your face... it was hot that one time. Because it was chocolate, and because you were totally unaware of it, and probably because I was a little drunk. Messy eating in general, that's not sexy. You know that, right? It just makes you look like...." He saw the expression on Caleb's face and his voice softened. "No, don't feel bad. I appreciate the effort." He paused. "It's kind of cute, really. I mean...." He leaned forward, low enough that he could look up into Caleb's downturned face. "It's kind of kissable, really." He paused, as if weighing his options, and then leaned a little farther. He brought his lips to Caleb's cheek, he darted his tongue out to catch the cream cheese. He brought it back to his mouth, smiled softly, and then flicked his tongue out again to catch any remains. "*You're* kind of kissable," he said, and his voice was husky. He slipped one hand inside Caleb's shirt, the backs of his fingers running over Caleb's ribs and up to his nipple, and Caleb smiled.

He'd won. It had been a cheap victory, because Caleb knew Peter could have held out a hell of a lot longer if he'd wanted to. But it was sweeter than a real win, in a way, because it hadn't been lust that had overcome Peter, but something much deeper and more important. Something worth sharing.

"I love you, Peter," Caleb said softly.

"You're damn right you do," Peter replied, and he pulled Caleb forward into a kiss that was just as demanding, just as strong and passionate as their first kisses had been. Peter pulled away long enough to say, "And I love you back, so... that works out pretty well."

Caleb gasped as Peter's mouth left his and found the sensitive spot under his ear, but he fought for control. "I guess we found our win-win solution," he said. And then Peter's mouth continued its path down his body, and he lost the ability, or the need, to form words.

"All part of the process," Peter agreed, and his smile was the most beautiful thing Caleb had ever seen. He'd lost a lot in the past few months, but he'd gained so much more. He braced a hand on the warm glass of the window and looked down at the man he loved, and he felt safe and happy. And the best part was that he knew Peter felt the exact same way.

ABOUT THE AUTHOR

Kate Sherwood, Cate Cameron, Catherine Dale... and probably a few new names, eventually. They're all one person.

One person who's lucky enough to get to live a bunch of extra lives through all the characters in her books, and who's trying desperately to keep all the lives organized into some sort of categories... so each name writes a different type of story.

But really, beneath the genre categories? All the stories will have some kind of humour, even in the darkest times. They'll all show characters who are far from perfect, but who are trying to be better.

Basic bio stuff? Kate/Cate/Catherine lives in Cottage Country, the water-filled world north of Toronto, Canada, the land where summers are sunny and crowded with visitors and winters are snowy and isolated. She loves it there. Not that she doesn't sometimes miss the city, especially when her internet is acting up or she wants something delivered!

She works full-time at a non-writing job but would love to shift into a more writing-centred life. There's a five-year plan. It might work....

OTHER BOOKS BY KATE SHERWOOD

For details, see www.booklives.com

Writing as Kate Sherwood (m/m)

All That Glitters – contemporary romance

Long Shadows, Embers, Darkness, Home Fires – four book contemporary action

Feral, Lap Dog, Twice Shy, Pure Bred – four book NA contemporary romance

Sacrati – fantasy/alt history

In Too Deep – NA contemporary romance

Chasing the Dragon – angst and adventure!

Mark of Cain – contemporary romance

The Fall, Riding Tall – two book contemporary romance

The Shift – contemporary fantasy novella – monster hunters!

Room to Grow – contemporary romance novella

The Pawn, The Knight – two book futuristic romance with plenty of angst

Poor Little Rich Boy – contemporary romance

More than Chemistry – light contemporary novella

Dark Horse, Out of the Darkness, Of Dark and Bright – three book contemporary romance with extras

Shying Away – NA romance

Lost Treasure – contemporary romance

Writing as Cate Cameron (m/f, YA)

The Billionaire's Forever Family – contemporary romance

Center Ice, Playing Defense, Winging It, Breakaway – contemporary YA hockey romance

Just a Summer Fling, Hometown Hero – contemporary small town romance

Shining Armor – contemporary romance (originally published under "Kate Sherwood")

Writing as Catherine Dale (YA, contemporary fantasy, general fiction—everything but romance!)

Dark Houses – Speculative YA